Dear Reader,

Although I was born and bred in Sydney, I always felt more at home in the country. I like the village I live in, but I flee to my Blue Mountains when I need to feel in touch with *me* again. I also love the red earth and untamed vastness of the outback. I've been privileged to visit Kakadu National Park, where much of *Crocodile Dundee* was filmed, and I fell in love with the spiritual vista of untouched creation, decorated only with Aboriginal paintings that tell centuries-old stories. I've also been to Mungo National Park, where the vast ocher sands shift over slow decades, and you feel insignificant in the magnificent silence. It is my hope to take my readers to these special places in future books...but I hope to give you a taste of outback life in each of my next few releases.

Laila and Jake are outback kids. And, as it did to me, the outback's vast silence takes them and won't let go. I hope you love their story—I write it from experience. To the many women who won't settle for less than a marriage of the heart, this story is for you.

Melissa James

Silence fell on them like the shimmering waves of late-afternoon summer heat. The quiet was tense, anxious. The anticipation sat on her like the aura of dry heat everywhere. Unable to stand it, she opened her eyes.

Jake just stared at her, as if she'd said something profound, or stunning.

"You don't need to worry about me," she insisted, feeling as if Jake were waiting for the rest of what she had to say. "Go on with your work. I'll be fine on my own."

The heat from his eyes hit her over and over. It zinged between them, a cloud of everything he'd left unspoken…and the woman in her—ripened with the hormones of pregnancy, melting with memory of their one bittersweet night, and on high alert since the kiss they'd shared—ached with wanting. He hadn't wanted just any woman that night, he'd wanted *her*.… "Why did you leave me like that?" she whispered.

His gaze burned on her a moment longer, before he turned away with startling abruptness. "I had my reasons." Knife-edged as the land outside in its harshness, his voice tore into her hopes and fears with a serrated edge.

MELISSA JAMES
Outback Baby Miracle

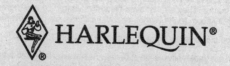

HARLEQUIN®

TORONTO • NEW YORK • LONDON
AMSTERDAM • PARIS • SYDNEY • HAMBURG
STOCKHOLM • ATHENS • TOKYO • MILAN • MADRID
PRAGUE • WARSAW • BUDAPEST • AUCKLAND

ISBN-13: 978-0-373-03936-4
ISBN-10:   0-373-03936-0

OUTBACK BABY MIRACLE

First North American Publication 2007.

www.eHarlequin.com

Printed in U.S.A.

Melissa James is a mother of three, living in a beach suburb in New South Wales, Australia. A former nurse, waitress, shop assistant, perfume and chocolate demonstrator, among other things, she believes in taking on new jobs for the fun experience. She'll try anything at least once to see what it feels like—a fact that scares her family on regular occasions. She fell into writing by accident, when her husband brought home an article stating how much a famous romance author earned, and she thought, *I can do that!* She can be found most mornings walking and swimming at her local beach with her husband, or every afternoon running around to her kids' sporting hobbies, while dreaming of flying, scuba diving, belaying down a cave or over a cliff—anywhere her characters are at the time!

Just like having a heart-to-heart with your best friend, these stories will take you from laughter to tears and back again!

Curl up and have a

with
Harlequin® Romance

So heartwarming and emotional,
you'll want to have some tissues handy!

Look out for more stories in
HEART TO HEART
coming soon

Next month, don't miss
Their Very Special Gift
by Jackie Braun

PROLOGUE

Wallaby Station, Outback New South Wales

How do you tell a man who's never spared you a word beyond the occasional "G'day, miss" or "Nice day, Miss Robbins" that you can't stop thinking about him?

Especially when he wasn't one of the eager men surrounding her?

Laila excused herself with detached politeness. She'd walked away from eager men for most of the past seven years. Trouble was she'd never known, and probably would never know, if any of those men were attracted to her—or to her father's wealth and influence.

Brian Robbins had turned his grandfather's scraggly thousand acres, given to him as a returning soldier from World War One, into two distinct one hundred thousand acre empires, with prize-winning racehorses and prime Angus cattle at the Hunter Valley enterprise, and the toughest Marino sheep here at Wallaby—and plenty of men wanted a piece of it.

At twenty-five, Laila thought she had no illusions left. The only men she trusted were Dar, and her brothers Andrew and Glenn. How many of their warnings had turned out to be true?

Then she'd seen *him*.

The man she kept her gaze on as she threaded through the

five hundred-thick crowd celebrating Dar and Marcie's fifteenth wedding anniversary.

He stood in a corner as bright-lit as the rest of the house, yet it seemed darker. She didn't know if it was because he was the only man here in his working clothes—the Outback working-man's uniform of worn jeans and plain cotton shirt, albeit clean—or the hint of a tortured soul hidden inside his masked expression.

He was hurting tonight. Hurting in a way far deeper than the usual curt withdrawal he used when he cut her off. He was hurting so badly he couldn't even hide it.

How she knew that, she wasn't sure—maybe because she spent so much time watching him. The fascination she'd felt from the first glance at him, straight-backed, black-haired and golden-eyed, sitting astride a horse like her girlhood dreams of a wild Cherokee warrior-lover, had only grown with every university break she'd come home. Even when she wasn't home, no man—student, fellow worker or customer at the restaurant—could compare.

It had been a year since then, and he'd said a total of ninety-seven words to her, sixty of those "G'day, miss." She couldn't stand it anymore. It was now or never. She had to know if this was infatuation without solid ground, or if it could be something real.

He didn't notice her approaching, and Laila wasn't even certain he'd seen her when she reached him apart from the way he drew deeper inside himself.

But she couldn't make herself leave him, not now, not when she was so sure he needed help…needed *her*. She drew in a deep breath for courage, and willed special, wonderful words to say that would make him know all the exquisite turmoil she felt…

"Want to talk about it? This is Dar and Marcie's happy occasion, but your gloomy face is enough to make the lot of us drown in your sorrows."

She cursed her clumsy mouth even before she finished. Why could she never say what she felt inside? Why were her words always blunt-spoken when it meant so much to get it *right*?

Then she realized he hadn't even heard. He was staring into nothing, the bronzed skin of his slanted cheeks taut, hands clenched so tight around the schooner of beer he'd obviously forgotten the glass might shatter any moment.

"Let me take that for you." Gently she prised his fingers from their death grip on the glass, and put it out of reach.

Finally he turned to her. The look on his face wasn't a scowl, or the dark, withdrawn politeness of everyday wear. Those haunting, dark golden eyes were wild, blank—*blinded* with everything he held inside. He looked at her, but he didn't see her.

Wrapped in blackness, his pain screamed all the stronger in its silence.

"Jake?" she whispered, and touched his hand.

He didn't move, didn't speak. It was as if he couldn't—then she felt it. He was *shaking*.

"Come with me. Let me help you," she whispered. Slowly, terrified because reaching out to him, touching him *meant* so much, she cupped her palm to his cheek. Overwhelmed, exultant, fragile with hope. *Please, please let me in...*

The look he gave her was still blinded, still *lost*. He lifted a hand as if he didn't know what he did, and touched her jaw, cheek and nose as if he truly had no sight: a man reaching out from behind dank prison bars, starved of human touch. Her head slowly fell back as she drank in not sensuality, but *need*. The savage, hopeless need of a man so long alone, he'd forgotten the power of a simple touch.

Did he even know who she was? She doubted it—yet it didn't matter. He *needed* her because she'd reached out at the right moment—and she had to make that be enough for now.

"Please, Laila, just get me out of here," he whispered, eyes closed, face in agony.

Joy and sorrow burst together within her. *He knew her. He needed her.*

She took his hand and led him out of the room.

CHAPTER ONE

Two months later

SHE had to tell him.

From the corner of a shadowed stall, Laila watched him—
her man, if only she could get him to see her, talk to her, to
listen for longer than twenty seconds. But those incredible,
amber-gold eyes were filled with shadows, even beneath his
Akubra hat. He was stalking into the barn, a mug in one hand
and a letter in the other.

Jake Connors never simply walked anywhere. Nothing he
did was simple. He moved around Wallaby Station as if chased
by a horde of demons. He wore his intensity like a second skin:
a storm cloud flicking tiny bolts of lightning, never allowing
it to fully unleash.

Even after that night, and his abrupt desertion of her bed
before sunrise, making it clear ever since that he wanted to
forget what happened between them, something about him
called to the woman in her in a way no other man ever had.

Would he speak to her this time? Would he finally meet her
eyes?

My hands are shaking.

Excitement, terror, the deep, craving ache wouldn't go

away—for him, only for him. Without even trying, Jake Connors had turned her into a woman she didn't recognize.

Where had her stubborn independence gone, all her pride in making her life work her way? Laila Robbins didn't need a man to make her complete—she could do it on her own. Growing up the baby of the family, with two older brothers and a father fiercely overprotective of his only daughter, she knew how it felt to be stifled in a man's world.

Thank heaven Dar had chosen his second wife wisely. Within days of their marriage, Marcie became the mother Laila could barely remember. By the time Laila was eighteen, Marcie's influence had led her to an independent life in Bathurst, with a job all her own, her choice of study…and Dar and the boys giving her a measure of distance. If not for Marcie, she knew one or another of them would be on her doorstep every weekend, vetting her life, her job, friends, the men looking at her—making certain she got it right. Their little girl couldn't be allowed to hurt, to feel, to experience life like normal girls.

She was the Robbins princess—and she couldn't be allowed out of the ivory tower.

Laila adored her stepmother for giving her space—and dignity. Marcie let her *live* her life, her way, without Dar and the boys constantly in her face, filling her life to overflowing. Marcie had taught her to exercise her independence, and hang on to it against all odds. Never would she be subjugated to a man's will, a man's anxiety, ever again.

Yet from the day Jake Connors came to Wallaby to jackaroo at her father's massive Outback sheep property, a self-contained man, with depths he let no one explore, she'd felt the change begin. Curiosity soon became fascination with the first tipping of his hat and polite greeting. He knew who she was, and didn't care…

When fascination had become enthrallment, she wasn't

certain; she was lost inside it before she could stop it, and he didn't even have a clue.

Even now, a year and two months since they met—even when she was hundreds of miles away attending university—he was always there in her mind. His amber-gold eyes lived as a separate entity in her imagination; his hands and lips that had given her—*what*? Deeper than ecstasy, stronger and more binding than physical bliss, he'd somehow wound himself insidiously around her heart like a vine, holding on with a tenacity she couldn't fight or deny.

And the anguished need he'd shown for her that night had made the girl a woman on a far deeper level than anything their bodies had done.

Being with Jake was everything she'd never even dreamed of. Exquisite, almost unbearable in its poignancy…and unforgettable. She dreamed of their loving, but more, she dreamed of *him*. She ached, burned and wished, less for a return of the physical beauty he'd given her than for that which eluded her, before that night and ever since—the essence of the real man inside.

One night of bliss, followed by months of misery. Was it worth it? She honestly couldn't say…

Was this love? She didn't know, but to have any form of life from now on, she had to find out; and for the sake of the life growing inside her, she needed to know her baby's father.

He'd barely spoken a word to her that night; but then, she hadn't needed him to talk. His anguish had been a living, pulsing thing, so searing and vivid that mere words would have cheapened it. He'd turned to her, needing comfort, and she'd melted. Five years of cynical resistance faded with a single touch, turning a crush, an infatuation into—

She was terrified to name what she felt for Jake, but was too honest with herself to lessen her emotion. No man had ever done so much to her without asking anything back.

That night, she'd discovered the heady power of the silent man, and the compelling magnetism of all he left unspoken. He hadn't thought about her wealth or her family name, or her inheritance: he didn't *care* about those things. She had to know that. He'd never once tried to hit on her, even when he must have known, must have *seen* her absolute and utter fascination with him, her inability to see any man but him.

No. That night he'd needed *her,* as no man had before. The sweetest aphrodisiac she'd ever known. But he'd refused to look at her since his awkward apology the morning after that one glorious night. For the past two months he wouldn't speak to her, or mention her name.

Was it his fear of that need repeating that had him on the run now?

She hoped to heaven that she was right…because now she needed *him,* needed him to be there for her as she'd been for him that single, exquisite night; and if he didn't want her—if she had just been a female body—the biggest gamble of her life would fail.

Absolution and redemption didn't come cheap to any man; and though it might come in time for some, as far as John Jacob Sutherland was concerned, never was too soon for him. Yet here it was again, another chance at forgiveness he could barely stand to read, let alone accept. Not after what he'd done—or what he hadn't done.

How am I supposed to forget that I killed my wife?

Leaning against the cold, dark wall of the barn, a pitchfork in his hand and two scraps of paper in the other, his half-congealed cup of coffee on the slat rail long forgotten, Jake reread his sister's latest letter that came to him via the faceless lawyer in Sydney.

Dear Jake,

    I pray this letter reaches you safely. Please, just write

to me or call, and let me know you're alive and well? Five years and not one word—it hurts, Jake, especially now Dad's gone. Burrabilla feels empty without you here. Aaron feels the same. He loves Burrabilla but it was always yours. It just feels wrong here without you.

I have to tell you, Mum came home a few months ago, and she's here to stay. I know you won't be happy about it, but she needs to be here, and Aaron and I want her. Please don't think it's because you didn't do a good job raising us—you did—but she's our mother, and there are reasons she left, apart from what Dad told us. She'd like to see you, to make things right.

Please, Jake, come home. I'm sure Bill and Adah don't blame you for what happened—or Darren, either. Jenny wouldn't want you to do this to yourself. I know she wouldn't, she was my best friend. She'd want you to be happy. I know you feel responsible for what happened, but weren't we all? We all left her there that day.

Please, just one call, one letter. Is that too much to ask of my brother? We love you. We miss you. I miss you.
Sandy

Jake closed his eyes, gripping the two sheets of paper so hard in his hands they tore down the middle, wishing to God that he could close off his heart, his memories, with such ease. Though it was late winter, the sweat on his brow beaded, banded together and trickled down his face. Slowly he pulled off his Akubra, and the wide-brimmed hat fell to the floor with the pieces of the destroyed letter as he wiped shaking hands on dirty, dusty jeans.

So his mother had come home, after twenty-six years, seeking forgiveness. It seemed Sandy and Aaron had already given it. Fair enough; Mum had gone when they were only seven. They didn't remember their dad's utter heartbreak. They hadn't had to fit school in their spare time while they ran the place, until Dad finally gave up hoping Mum would come back, and hired a housekeeper.

So she wanted to make things right…he felt something like hysterical laughter bubbling up inside. How can you undo the past? How do you make the worst of wrongs come right? Maybe she had some answers for him. God knows he needed some answers on the subject—but then, her sins hadn't killed anyone.

Jake slumped against the wall of the tack room, letting his back slide down the splintery wood until his butt hit solid ground. He could sit a while. It was "smoke-oh" time at Wallaby Station, in the fertile Riverina area southeast of Broken Hill.

"Smoke-oh" was the time of day that city people called morning tea. Jenny had called it morning tea, even though she'd grown up on the land. Three years in Brisbane had taken some of the Outback out of the girl—until Jake had met his sister's old friend again, fell for her, courted and married her inside of a month. He'd taken his bride to Burrabilla, the Sutherland Outback property for four generations. Jenny was queen to his king. He'd felt as if he owned the world back then, with a gorgeous bride to prove it.

"Smoke-oh" became "morning tea" for the year that Jenny ruled her Outback palace; but by the time their first anniversary came around, she was dead.

Now he owned nothing, wanted nothing. He was a jackaroo, an almost thirty-eight-year-old common worker in the Outback, rounding up sheep, riding fences, caring for the horses and livestock. This was all the future he had the right to expect, and "smoke-oh" was good enough for the likes of him.

He had ten minutes to pull himself together before the guys came looking for him. If they saw him looking like he'd been stretched over a burning-hot rack, they'd want to know why. These rough, kindhearted guys let him have his solitude most of the time, sensing his need to be alone, but they'd never leave him in this kind of agony.

He didn't deserve their concern. He wasn't worthy of the welcome home Sandy hinted about in the letter. Jenny's parents Bill and Adah couldn't have forgiven him. He couldn't face the hand of friendship Jenny's brother Darren might extend to him—because if he searched for the rest of his life he wouldn't find any echo of redemption inside his own soul.

He had blood on his hands, because he'd been too busy to *hear* Jenny when she'd said her back felt strange that morning. He'd offered to stay home, but even he'd heard the halfheartedness, the impatience in his voice. Surely it was only the weight of the baby pressing against her back? His mind had been on getting the cattle to market for the yearling sales.

Jenny had smiled and said she'd be fine; the baby wasn't due for eight weeks. It was probably just stretching discomfort, and a bit of bending and stretching to paint the bottom of the nursery walls would help.

He'd nodded, relieved; though he loved Jenny deeply, and was excited about their coming child, he'd had a cattle muster on his mind. He'd have all the time in the world for his family in just a few days…and meanwhile, the bit of room arranging she wanted to do wouldn't hurt. A little bit of nesting would keep her busy while he was gone.

Now every muster time half killed him with the memory of what might have been. He shouldn't have gone. He should never have left her. Banning her from climbing ladders hadn't been enough. If she hadn't climbed the chair to hang a baby mobile because he'd been too busy thinking of profit-loss and the stupid *cattle*…

So now he didn't do muster: he didn't work with cattle at

all. Sheep were his business now…no, they were Brian
Robbins's business. He just worked here.

He jammed on his hat, picked up the crumpled pieces of
Sandy's letter and walked through to the main barn. He
grabbed the pitchfork, shoved the torn shreds on it, and pitched
the shredded remains of his sister's loving forgiveness deep
into the heart of the drying hay bale. Loving, wishing—*regret*.
All the love and wishing in the world couldn't undo the past.

Time to get back to work. The one thing he took solace
in—he loved the hard work entailed in keeping a massive
property running.

"That won't get rid of her, you know."

He froze, but behind him the amused voice—a voice whose
soft breathiness he'd spent months trying to ram out of his
memory—carried on.

"Women aren't so easy to put behind you. You can walk
away, but the memory remains to haunt you, like a bad smell
you can't get off your shoes. You can hose it off, but just when
you think it's all washed away, it comes rising up again to
remind you of where you've been."

He swung around, pitchfork still in his hands, wielding it
before him like a physical shield against the probing of his
wounds. She was the voice of his conscience, a memory that
should never have happened—and she was about to twist a
knife only she knew existed.

Or did everyone know what he'd done? He could barely
remember a thing before she'd taken him outside—and up to
her room. Everyone in the local area could know what
happened. The guys had definitely treated him with more re-
spectful wariness since the party…

She stepped out of the shadows of an empty stall, jean-clad
and booted, hat in hand, into the aureole of sunshine spilling
from the skylight above. Her hair, a bright, burnished auburn,
glowed like a warm halo around her. And that impudent grin

of hers lit up her lightly tanned, pretty face. This girl had the world on a plate, and she knew it.

"Hello, Jake Connors. How unusual, you're hiding out in the barn at break time. Sociable creature, aren't you?"

Connors was the name he'd gone by for the past five years. It seemed fitting at the time, taking Jenny's maiden name, living the life she'd lost; yet it felt like a sick lie, coming from the lips of this pretty, vital girl, who'd broken his five-year barriers with a touch.

Laila Robbins made him *feel* things he no longer had a right to, like sweetness and joy and *hope*. The shattered remnants of that night lived inside him still, leaving him unsure and ashamed to face her. If she knew the truth about his past, she wouldn't have come within a mile of him, let alone touched him.

His heart thudded in his chest. He couldn't smile at her, not when it felt like she could see right through him to the hideous truth beneath his stoic silence. "G'day, miss. Nice to see you."

"You're such a liar—you've been avoiding me since I came home. And you know my name's Laila," she returned softly, those soft, silvery blue, twinkling eyes of hers sparkling with life—eating him up inside. "You called me Laila the night of Dar and Marcie's party."

That *amazing* night…the night he'd cursed himself for ever since.

Why had he ever let himself get bludgeoned into attending the anniversary bash, only a day before the fifth anniversary of Jenny's death? He'd seen the girl's eyes lingering on him whenever he was near her—and she was close to him too often for his peace of mind.

And he found himself looking back at her *far* too often. He didn't know why she was different to every other woman; he only knew she dragged his gaze to her like a dumb fish to a death lure. She wasn't prettier than those women, or more feminine. She was just Laila, straight-shooting Outback girl, impudent and strong, innocent and wise, with eyes that saw straight through his unbreakable façade…as she had that night, and gave him the comfort that led to a night he'd never forget…and forever regret.

He'd woken the next morning to the anniversary he'd do anything not to have in his life—and he'd spent the night in another woman's arms. *Jenny, darlin', I'm so sorry!*

He'd betrayed her all over again because he didn't have any self-control when it came to this sassy-mouthed redhead with insights that made him uncomfortable and yearn at once.

If there was one thing he knew, it was that Laila Robbins wasn't the kind of girl to play around. If he hadn't noticed the deep, emotional innocence beneath the woman's ready body and her bubbly, teasing nature at first, he'd known it when he'd made love to her. Though she wasn't a virgin, there was no way this girl knew the score, or how it went with guys like him.

Her adoring father and brothers' nickname for her, "Princess," had been broadcast to the world via the bush tele-graph of jackaroos' gossip. It suited her. She was fair and pretty, in a fresh-faced, outdoor-girl way, with a rich, unconscious femininity in her hip-swinging walk. Smart as a whip, she was studying veterinary science. She was small in stature, yet more than made up for it with her wilful ways, a bundle of repressed energy, irrepressible and outspoken. Why all that made her gorgeous he didn't know, but all the local guys had the hots for her—

But since the disaster of a party night, he knew better than to think about her at all. So what if it had been the most—the *only*—beautiful thing to happen to him in five years? He was an angry, jaded thirty-eight to her fresh-and-shining twenty-five or -six. She had a future; he didn't even want a past.

Laila's fresh, freckled prettiness was nothing like Jenny's exotic golden-brown beauty, yet she was like Jenny in her heart. Laila had talked to him, held him—loved him as if he'd *mattered*. She'd seen beneath the shell of ice he'd put around himself to find the isolated, despairing man within...

"Well?"

At the impudent word, he wheeled away from her tempting scent of sunshine and earth surrounding her like an aura. He hung the pitchfork back up on its safety rack. "I have to get back to work."

"Didn't your mother teach you better manners than that?" Her voice had a gentle, husky touch to it. "First you say 'welcome home, Laila.'"

His mother? He could barely remember when she'd stopped fighting with Dad long enough to teach him anything—and she'd taken off before he'd hit his teens. "Welcome home, miss." He brushed past without touching her. "Have a nice stay."

"Jake." She put a hand on his arm as he stalked out.

It stopped him midstride, like a road train jackknifed in half. The honesty inside that touch—the vulnerability she didn't hide—hurt him somewhere deep down. A place he hadn't allowed to be touched in five years.

A place only Jenny had ever touched before.

She lifted her face, her shining eyes searching his in the warm half-light of the barn. She looked so fresh and pretty that he wanted to snarl, to jerk his arm from her hold, but years of control held firm. "Yes, miss?"

"Just one thing," she said softly. "Do you mean to avoid me for the rest of your life? Is that a message, Jake? Was I just a girl for the night...a way to ease the pain?"

Trust Princess Laila to get right to the heart of the matter—but he couldn't tell her she was wrong, that he hadn't even been able to *look* at another woman since that night. She'd brought warmth to his life, like a burst of summer sunshine reaching the deepest Antarctic, and he wanted, craved more—

Day and night, he craved to touch her, hold her—to betray Jenny's memory yet again with this girl. *Only* this girl.

Jake shook her off before his will broke, aching to taint her luminous innocence with dark, destructive desire that could only hurt her, because he had nothing left to give. "I'm the wrong guy to play games with."

She put her hands on her hips and smiled. "Who says I'm playing games?" Her voice held all the husky promise he'd tried like hell not to dream of since that night.

He turned on her, fire and churning fear in his gut. *She's here again. She keeps coming back, even though I avoid her to the point of rudeness. God help me if she has feelings for me!*

Her starry blue eyes filled his vision. Her body's warmth touched his skin, and temptation hit him with a hard wallop. Temptation to take everything he knew she was offering.

"I say you're playing," he growled. "And I say you're stupid to even think about me."

Her smile slipped a little. A flash came and went in her eyes; and for all that she was small and fair, he saw Jenny's face that final day, so valiantly hiding her fear and need for him to stay home while he'd had his mind on muster. *We'll go away when I get back, okay, darlin'? I'll call you three times a day, I promise.*

By the second call Jenny was bleeding, a wild storm had broken, and the Flying Doctors couldn't land the plane—and he was a two-hour drive from her. When he'd found her, she was unconscious, and it was too late for both mother and daughter.

"Go away, little girl," he grated, harsh with the emotional and sensual roller coaster he'd been on this morning. "Find a nice boy to flirt with, a kid who'll let you take your time in becoming a woman."

"I *am* a woman, Jake. You know that." She was soft and provocative, her smile so sweet, his white-hot reaction to her almost sickened him. "I'm old enough to decide whom I want to spend time with. I've lived away from home for seven years."

"You're a baby," he shot back. God help him, he had to get her away from him, *now*. "You're a protected little princess who likes touching her fingers to the fire. But I'm your worst bushfire. I won't give you flowers and nice words, promises and a diamond ring. I'll take you for an hour, maybe a day or two, and then I'll forget you existed. And when you go crying to Daddy, you'll know just how much of a kid you still are." He stood over her, facing her down, and waited for the inevitable reaction.

She gasped and whirled away, her cheeks burning, and the regret at hurting her so badly seared him right through—but he steeled himself against the apology he ached to make. *Run away, Laila Robbins. Go and find a nice, safe life without me anywhere in it.*

"Fine," she muttered, her sweet voice strangled. "But don't tell me to run, because it's *you* who's running. You're the coward! I'm sorry I ever thought you needed a friend, or—or hoped we could…and I'm sorry I'm—"

She sounded all ripped up inside. Yeah, he'd torn her ego into pieces like he'd shredded Sandy's letter minutes before.

He ached to put the smile back on her face, take her in his arms, and kiss her like he had that night. But he couldn't. Hurting her pride now was better than giving in to this madness, and tossing another sweet, hope-filled life on the emotional scrap heap.

"Don't be sorry, just go," he said, fighting with his own throat to stop the words coming out with any gentleness or apology. *Please, just go…*

She dashed at her eyes with the back of her hand. "Have you been alone, hiding from the real life so long that the thought of a woman reaching out to you terrifies you?"

Her unwanted insight made the lump in Jake's chest expand

until it felt like he'd explode. But when she wheeled back, her eyes tear-bright with the humiliation he'd put her through, he knew she hadn't finished. He had to grit his teeth to stop the apology from escaping his lips.

"I just wanted to know you," she said, her voice unnaturally calm considering the lingering shadows of pain in her star-bright eyes. "I wanted to see the man beneath the ice, to know if—" Her cheeks flushed again, and her eyes blazed. "But you push me away like you push everyone else, never talking to anyone, living in the shadows like a criminal on the run. You've got what you wanted...but don't kid yourself that you're safer this way. You'll live the rest of your life alone, you'll live alone and you'll *die* alone!"

She stumbled out of the enormous double doors, back to the sunlight where she belonged. Back to Bathurst and her studies, to a life with a future.

If she was smart, she'd never come within fifty feet of him ever again.

From the shadows of a barn grown suddenly dark and cold, Jake watched her go, trying to believe he'd done the right thing, for her sake.

But it didn't *feel* right. He'd just had another brief glimpse of the sweet sunshine warmth Laila took with her wherever she went—and she'd snatched it from him because he'd forced her to. Because he was too old and scarred and angry and *scared* for a woman like Laila.

One night with her was far more than he'd deserved. All he'd given her was *this*. Pain and humiliation. He was all wrong for her, and he always would be.

Now he had no choice but to melt back into the cold, dark shadows he'd walked in the past five years, and he'd stay there until the day he died.

CHAPTER TWO

Almost three months later

THIS was ridiculous, spending hours hiding out in the barn, grooming the horses.

She shouldn't even be at Wallaby. Wasn't this what she'd been running from since the time she'd graduated high school? From her teen years, she'd fought the loving smothering of Dar and the boys, who saw her as fragile and in need of their constant care, instead of the tough Outback woman she was. She loved her family dearly, but she wished they could see how much they held her down by rescuing her from every one of life's emotional bumps and falls.

If she'd had anywhere else to go, she'd have gone. Bathurst was no longer an option: throwing up day and night hadn't left much room for final-year studies. And since that stage ended, her constant tiredness and unpredictable emotional state didn't gel with hours spent on her feet waitressing and dealing with the cheerful or obnoxious drunks that came to the steakhouse next to the university.

Faced with inevitability, she'd ached for home, for her family—but they hadn't stopped invading her space from the day she'd arrived with all her bags. Even Marcie was crowding her, asking day and night what was wrong, and if she could help.

Well, they're worried because they don't know why I came home just before my semester exams. Any family would be!

Wallaby didn't seem like home anymore: it had become the place where *he* was.

The father of my child...a man I don't even know.

Laila couldn't bear to see him. She knew if she were as smart and strong as she pretended to be, she'd get out of here, leave his memory behind her, find another man, and wash this one right out of her hair.

She'd tried to do that, oh, *how* she'd tried...but even if she'd met a man who fascinated her the way Jake Connors did, she had a daily reminder of their unwilling connection, his humiliating rejection of her. The baby was currently giving her butterfly kisses from inside her womb; and despite her downright terror at the inevitable changes to her life plan, she couldn't help smiling, and caressing the tiny mound.

My baby.

After months of struggling to keep her pregnancy quiet, she'd lost her job by taking too many days off or coming late to work because she'd fallen asleep again. Then, needing somewhere to belong when Bathurst was no longer a viable option, she'd come home like some hurt creature, hiding out in darkened corners, licking her wounds.

Yet deep inside, with all her stupid, hopeful heart, she knew she'd been praying that sooner or later he would notice her—that he'd *care* enough to notice her body's change, since she'd begun to show, and connect the dots.

What happened to all her pride in herself, all her independence?

Jake Connors happened.

Yeah, that...or rather, he was the crux of the matter. All

these years she'd thought she'd been experiencing life; now she knew she'd only floated. Oh, it hadn't been easy. She'd studied hard, worked long hours, and got what she wanted without the backup of the loving, protective father whose enormous shadow she'd fought so hard to escape, especially with men. Men who'd connected her surname to her father, and hoped to get a ride on the gravy train through her.

People look at you because you're a Robbins. Guys want to date you because you're a Robbins. You can't expect a guy to just ignore that, unless he's as filthy rich as you are.

That day, her life changed forever. She couldn't even remember the guy's name, but his words were unforgettable. It was the day her illusions—or rather, *de*lusions—shattered. People, not just men, did look at her as a Robbins, not as a person. Every good exam grade she made had to have been a bought mark; every mistake she made, she was playing the Princess—or soon would, to remain consequence-free. It didn't matter that she'd never once done any of it. She wasn't normal, had never been normal, and that was a part of life she had to accept.

Since then, she hadn't even dared to do the normal university student things, like getting plastered at parties—or getting plastered anywhere. She had enough trouble being taken seriously without letting a single spot ruin what reputation for intelligence she had.

But taking the high ground felt so lonely at times. Oh, she had friends—all three of them. Danni, Jodie and Jimmy. They knew her, loved and accepted her for the person they knew. But with everyone else she felt different, set apart, watched by others, not for *who* she was, but *what* she was. She didn't dare believe she'd ever meet the kind of man she'd dreamed of since childhood—a country boy who shared her love of the Outback and its wild creatures, and would want her without caring what her last name was.

Then in the last place she'd thought to look, she'd seen a man on a horse: a quiet Outback cowboy with the remote, beautiful face, and her deep, long-hidden dreams of womanhood came to the fore. She couldn't get Jake Connors out of her mind, or stop her body aching for what she'd never known. Cold as ice, mystery trailing behind him, a loner existing in silence—how she'd dreamed that, if he'd only give her a chance, she could heal him of what haunted him.

But with a few words, her delusions exploded in her face for a second time, and with a much higher price than the first time.

Stop thinking about it.

How much chance did she have of that? She was beginning to show. She had to tell someone…everyone.

No—she had to tell *him*. But until she had the right words to say, until she could think of anything but blurting out *I'm pregnant*, she stayed out here with the horses.

Ironic, that the one person she wanted to avoid, the person she had to talk to, the one person she wanted to care enough to ask what was wrong, was the only one at Wallaby Station giving her any peace and space…

Stupid! He was never going to ask, never going to care. Why did she still want him to? Why did some crazy part of her keep hoping that she'd been right last time and it was fear of his feelings for her that made him so harsh, rather than the cold indifference she knew it to be?

It was the quietness of her sobbing that got to him.

When he'd heard the Princess was back from college, it was easy enough to avoid her. He wondered why she was home when her exams must be about to begin—but she wasn't talking to anyone—or so he'd heard.

When he'd heard the gossip—not even he could avoid all of it—that she'd become quiet and withdrawn, he stayed right away. He had enough to do, worrying about fifteen head of Brian Robbins's valuable Merino sheep that had been lost somewhere on the hundred-thousand-hectare property for the past week. Riding fences every day in the blazing cloudless sky under an early summer sun was no one's idea of joy, even for a man who preferred being alone. All that space gave a man no choice but to think, to remember.

When she started hiding out for hours each day in the barn, taking over young Colin's job of grooming the horses instead of riding them as she usually did, he let her invade his sanctum. He had his coffee in the shade under the eaves of the roof outside and ignored her, or rode fences when she did her thing.

It became a daily ritual: let's see who could avoid each other better.

If she wanted to prove she could go where she wanted, tossing him off his turf, that was fine. She wouldn't be here at Wallaby long enough for it to be a problem. And no one else needed to know that at night, he went over the spots she'd missed, or cleaned up the tack. The Princess had a problem and needed space—that was okay. He respected other people's need for solitude, and he didn't need much sleep, anyway. He could do the work at night after she'd sat in the stalls all afternoon, trying to sort herself out.

After their last meeting, he'd be the last person she'd suspect was covering for her.

The half-muffled sounds coming from inside the stifling warmth of the barn weakened his resolution—then destroyed it. In her attempts to remain quiet, she sounded so sad—so utterly lonely. It was as if something, or someone, had ripped apart that amazing, bright-as-the-sun spirit of hers, and left, not just her ego, but her whole heart, broken.

Laila Robbins, *broken*? The girl with the smile like living sunshine and a soul of a wild brumby, was sobbing as if her heart was torn into shreds?

Before he could think it through, Jake strode into the stall where Laila had taken to hiding, determined to sort this out—but at the sight of her, he all but tripped over his booted feet. Her bright hair, loose and tangled, spilled into the mane of the horse she was clutching on to as if her life depended on it. The currycomb was clenched in a hand whose knuckles strained white. Her lithe body was spasming with the sobs she was trying so hard to muffle.

So typically Laila that, even crying her heart out, she remained standing, keeping her pride and strength intact.

"Laila," he said quietly, keeping a careful distance. "If I could hear you from outside, others will, too."

With a gasping hiccup, the sobs stopped. Her face, pretty even while it was blotched and swollen, lifted from the mane—but she wouldn't look at him. "Sorry I bothered you."

It wasn't in any way an apology. Jake didn't flinch, even though the harsh, bitter tone of her voice shocked him. "You did bother me—but I assume you don't want others to know, which is why you keep coming here to groom the horses. You want to talk about it?"

"I'm fine, thanks. Please *go*," she muttered, her voice grating him with its raw pain.

He had no idea why he kept pushing after she'd given him an out, but he did. "You should speak to someone if it's upsetting you for this long. You want me to get your father?"

All vestiges of color drained from her face. He had an absurd impulse to snatch her into his arms, in case she fainted. "No."

"Andrew or Glenn, then?" He couldn't leave her like this. Someone ought to be here for her, and she seemed close to her brothers.

"No." She brushed her damp, tangled hair back from her face. "I just indulged in a weak moment. We all have them. You can leave now with a clean conscience. I'm fine."

Obviously she wasn't, but she wanted him to leave her alone—and he would have, but for the warning screaming inside him, *don't walk away.*

He circumnavigated the pitchfork lying between them like an impassive gauntlet, and sat down on the hay bale. "Looks like I'm it, then—supposing that you do need to talk to someone."

How ironic. He'd given her the opening she'd been praying for, at the very moment she was least ready. Was it Murphy's Law, or what? Slowly, Laila straightened her spine, and forced back the choking ball of fear in her throat; she would *not* cry in front of him! She had to tell him!

Her mind wiped of everything but two words.

She scrabbled around in her mind for something less dangerous. "You don't talk like the other jackaroos." She sat down on the other side of the bale, needing distance from him, needing to think. "You're obviously an educated man. You haven't been an Outback worker for very long, have you?"

She saw the half-wry, wary look shutter his eyes. "Long enough."

"You want me to talk, but you never talk about yourself." Her head tilted as she surveyed him. "You like being a mystery."

He shrugged, his face closing off even more. "Nothing to tell."

She gave an exaggerated sigh, her mind still racing. *Tell him, tell him, just say it!* "Of course there isn't. That's why you hide everything about yourself. You never talk about your life, your family and friends—if you have any. You barely talk to anyone on the station, have never left or had a visitor, yet you've been here over a year now." Her brows lifted in speculation.

He shifted on the hay, as if she'd found the proverbial needle in this bale and kept stabbing him with it. "Do you want to keep asking me questions I won't answer, or talk about why you were crying? Or will I go away and let you cry in peace?"

She chewed on her lip, knowing he wouldn't give her another opening.

She dragged in a deep breath, lifted her chin and met his gaze, desperately hiding her fear, hoping against hope he'd react well to the news. "I'm pregnant."

Did that sound angry? Aggressive? Did I sound stupid? Well, I'm a twenty-six-year-old woman who's pregnant by a man who doesn't even like me. Of course I'm stupid.

She closed her eyes for a moment, hoping, *praying* that he'd see through her attempt at pride and bravado to the terrified young woman inside, needing someone to care, some support—

She unclouded her vision and looked at him again, to gauge his reaction. Unfortunately, for once, it wasn't hard to interpret. He'd gone so pale she thought he might fall down. He drew in a breath, in obvious shock. "It's mine, isn't it?"

Did he even *need* to ask that? Did he think so little of her? "Do you think your *'sorry'* and bolting out the door the next morning left me with enough confidence to find another lover?" she asked, weary of dancing around the truth.

A long silence. Then, sounding unsteady, as if someone had walloped him in the head with a baseball bat—well, maybe she had—he said, "That's why you came to me a few months ago. You were going to tell me then."

Her jaw clenched. She didn't need to answer. She barely even knew why she was telling him about the pregnancy now. It wasn't as if he cared.

Jake knew from her aggression and silence he'd botched it, badly. Seeing the incident in the barn with the twenty-twenty vision of hindsight, he knew she must have been scared half to death. She'd tried to get him to talk first, so she could be sure it was safe to tell him about the baby…and he'd ripped her hopes to shreds, leaving her with months of fear and loneliness.

Calculating in his head, he knew she must be almost five

months pregnant—and judging by the silence on her state, her unwillingness to talk to her family, he was the first to know.

She'd been alone with this for months. He'd let her down, just as he'd let Jenny down. Worse, he'd acted like a world-class jerk. The poor kid had been shouldering this burden alone for five months because he'd driven her away.

Guilt and anguish clobbered him. "I'm sorry, I'm so *sorry*."

"I'm sure you're sorry. Sorry you ever touched me." She wheeled away, and the vision of Jenny shattered haunted him. This was Laila, and he'd hurt her as well. "Well, stop worrying. I don't want anything from you. I'll have him myself, and I'll bring him up myself."

"Like blazes you will," he snarled, surprising himself with the force of his sudden anger. "I have a say in this. This is my child."

Like an avenging fury she turned back on him, her eyes flashing. "Yes, and I'm his mother, and you don't even like me. If I can't take the heat—in other words, your rudeness and arrogance, your coldness—how will a child cope? Do you know how to give the kindness and love he'll need from his father?" Her hand covered her belly in a protective motion. "I won't let you hurt my baby."

The way you hurt me. The words hung in the air, unspoken.

Then, at last, Jake looked at her, *really l*ooked, and saw what he hadn't wanted to see before—the delicate hollows beneath her eyes, the fragility so clear to see in the clenched fists and trembling mouth.

Had he hurt her so badly that day, or was it carrying the burden of her secret so long that had changed her so much?

Either way, it still meant this was his fault. He had to fix it.

"I never said I don't like you," he began—but her snort was eloquent testimony of her disbelief. How did he tell her, *it's myself I hate*? There was no way she'd believe it—not without hearing the truth.

The truth he'd never tell anyone.

"So that's why you came home?" he asked, for the sake of saying something, *anything*. God knows he had to find a way to connect to her.

"I've been throwing up, and sleeping a lot." That nonchalant shrug came again: a defence mechanism any fool could see through. She was terrified, but refused to break down in front of him. "I knew I wouldn't pass. I can't finish university next year, because I'll have the baby at the start of term. I won't ask anyone to take him for me while I study."

Feeling as if she was shutting a door in his face before he'd even knocked on it, he reminded her of his part in this. "You can ask me."

Her withering glance told him what she thought of his offer.

He tried again. "If you do want to go back, you can hire a nanny in Bathurst—"

"Right. With the family money, is that it? It's all easy for me." Her eyes flashed. "No, thanks. I'll do what I've done the past seven years. Manage on my own."

Jake felt his brows lift. Not one word of this choice gossip had reached him during his year at Wallaby Station. "Good for you."

But he'd obviously hit a raw nerve with her; her eyes still flashed hot with fury. "All these years, people called me the Princess, thinking I took Dar's money—but they're wrong." She stood before him, her hands on her hips and a brow raised in a question she already knew the answer to. "Why do you think I haven't finished my course at twenty-six?"

He felt the burning fill his cheeks at a question they both knew was mere rhetoric. She knew what he'd thought. Party time for the Princess. A two-year stint in Europe, maybe—taking time out to play, to enjoy her youth, and of course she'd use Daddy's money to get around.

"Why don't you tell me why?" he asked, to get her to open

up. She had to be able to talk to someone—anyone could see she was almost collapsing under her burdens.

But she pulled herself together, lifting her chin and facing him with quiet dignity. "How I manage my life is not your concern."

"Of course it's my concern," he grated. "I'm responsible for the—" he scrabbled around in his mind—what was another word for mess? "—dilemma you're in."

"You weren't exactly alone that night," she reminded him, but with a touch of acid in her voice. "I told you, this is my responsibility. I don't need you to control my life."

She was blocking him out. Why had she told him at all if she didn't want his help? He felt as if he was beating his head against the stall. What did she want from him—a declaration of love and an engagement ring he'd been hiding in his pocket? He barely knew her—and she didn't know him at all.

It was time they tried to find out something about each other—no, it was time *he* tried.

"Do you want the baby?" He felt awkward asking, but he had to start somewhere.

She gave a one-shouldered shrug, still defiant. "Of course I want the baby, even if I'm not married—but that's normal these days, right?"

He knew better than to believe her blithe attitude. Pregnant and unmarried was a real curveball for the conservative Robbins clan. Brian Robbins's only daughter should have had the fairy-tale wedding with all the trimmings long behind her before the requisite heir came.

Laila deserved the wedding and trappings before the heir. She'd done nothing but give to him—and he'd done nothing at all. Nothing.

He'd be expected to do the right thing by her, as soon as her state became known…and almost to his shock, he wanted that, too. His father had done the right thing by his mother, and because of that, he, Jake, had had a brother and sister, a home at Burrabilla, a heritage—a life outside the stifling city with a single mother struggling to make things work on her own.

His child deserved no less. He and Laila ought to be a family for the child's sake, raising him or her in a united way. And Laila would need his help to raise the child, finish her course and work—all the things he knew she'd struggle to do alone.

But knowing Brian Robbins, he'd be expected to present himself as a worthy partner for Brian's precious girl—which meant returning to his real identity. Brian would insist that he call his family, to have them all down for the engagement party—and he'd want Jake's real name and financial status before the engagement could even happen.

It seemed he was about to be exposed for the fraud he was. Only an uncaring father wouldn't care that Jenny and Annabel died because he hadn't taken enough care of them—and Brian Robbins adored Laila. He'd probably toss Jake's sorry butt off Wallaby faster than he could say "weekend visitation rights."

Yeah, Laila had certainly hitched her star to the wrong wagon. She'd lost the life she'd planned and worked for during the past seven years, because of him.

Suddenly he wanted to heave his guts. This was a nightmare—and none of it was Laila's fault. She'd thought him an ordinary man when she'd come to him, and he'd grabbed at her like a starving man faced with a sudden banquet. Lost in the past, he'd been desperate for human comfort, for touch—desperate for her—and now she was stuck with the consequences.

Well, she wouldn't be alone. He'd been the one to ruin her, but he'd be damned if he'd leave her alone to face the life he'd given her.

The words came past the boulder of shame and guilt lodged in his throat. The betrayal of Jenny's memory once again. "We'll get married as soon as possible."

At the offer that sounded ungracious and panicked even to

him, life flared in her. "How noble of you—but don't bother. I won't go on a lifelong guilt-trip with you. I made the bad decision to sleep with you. You're not responsible for me, or the baby."

Yeah, right. If she didn't want him to feel responsible for her pregnancy she shouldn't have told him, because he'd already sped past the earlier signpost of *You Did This To Her* Street, and was hurtling down the road to *Damnation* Alley.

Marriage was the only way to make things right for her, and for their child.

He tipped up her chin with gentle fingers, trying like crazy to ignore the feel of her skin under his hand—yeah, the sweet, silky cream he remembered. Peaches and cream...

He voiced what he'd suspected five months ago when he was bolting from her bed and saw the look on her face: about eight hours too late to recognize the hidden insecurity behind the radiance of her smile. "Somebody else hurt you, didn't they? Before me."

She shrugged. "No need to make a sob story out of it. I must have bad genetics for attraction to go through this twice."

Jake felt his eyes burning into hers—but her gaze bored straight back. She'd only had two men in her life—and good God, she counted their disaster as one time. She'd been that inexperienced? "Did I hurt you more than that guy did?" he asked grimly.

She closed her eyes for a moment before offering a tired smile, twisted with a bitterness he'd never seen inside her before. "He hung around for a few weeks, but took off after another rich girl when he realized I wasn't going to buy him a ticket for the Robbins gravy train." Her nostrils flared and her smile turned defiant again. "You cut and ran out on me after one night, but at least you were honest about not wanting me."

Put like that, he sounded as big a jerk as her first lover.

You were a jerk.

All the worst names for a man he'd ever learned during his

lifetime in the Outback came to mind, but he repressed them. He had work to do—harder work than riding any fence. After all he'd done to make her run in the opposite direction, he now had to bring her around. He'd get Laila to marry him. He had to make things right for her, not just for the baby.

"Don't tell me, you're thinking of ways and means to bring a wedding about," she mocked sweetly, walking straight into his thoughts and scattering them. "Relax, Jake. I only want acknowledgment that you're the father. And if he ever wants to meet you—"

Despite her insulting tone, he knew what she was really saying: she was offering him an easy out. All he need do at this point was walk away, and keep in touch—if he was the kind of loser who didn't care about what he'd done to her life.

But even if his stomach didn't churn at the thought of walking away from Laila and his child, if he didn't feel sick to his guts at the thought of deserting her to her fate, he knew she, *Laila*, would haunt him for the rest of his life…just as Jen haunted him still.

"No," he croaked. "I won't leave it like this. I'm responsible for this mess—"

Her whole body stiffened; her eyes flashed. *"I am not a mess, and neither is my baby."*

He wanted to whack his head against the side of the stall. Could he make things any worse? "I didn't say you were a mess, or the baby—just the situation we're in."

"You're not in anything." Laila got to her feet, her face mutinous. "You made your feelings clear—and I will *not* marry a man who feels forced to it for the sake of a child he thinks of as a *mess*. I want a man who loves *me* and is happy about our child!"

"What did you expect? We barely know each other." She was heading out by the time he was halfway through the sentence, but he was at the stall gate before she reached it, and held her arm to stop her. "Don't storm off like a kid. This is serious. We need to talk."

She sighed. "I can't exactly escape this, you know. I just need a break from that dark, cold face of yours."

"Seems to me you're the one with attitude right now," he muttered.

Her face, fierce and cold as she'd just claimed his to be, stared into his. "Give me one good reason why I shouldn't have an attitude, given your own."

Put like that, he couldn't think of one.

"You will marry me," he muttered. "If you hate me now, we can—"

"No." Her voice was utterly filled with conviction. "Don't offer me a marriage in name only. My friend Danielle's parents did that, and for as long as she can remember they've hated each other. They buy separate groceries, use the kitchen at different times and never talk except to snipe at each other. But neither one will leave the house, or be the one to walk out. Even since she moved out, they won't divorce *for her sake*. They've wrecked their lives, and screwed her up so badly she doesn't trust any man, but they 'did the right thing.' That isn't going to happen to my child. I won't have him grow up as scarred and untrusting as poor Danni!"

How could he possibly answer that? How did she have the ability to read his thoughts, to be able to show up every flaw in his arguments? "It doesn't have to be like that."

"It's already going that way. You haven't said my name once since I said the fatal words 'I'm pregnant.' In fact, you haven't said my name since you bolted from the bed that morning." Tears hovered in her eyes, hanging stubbornly on her lashes, but she wouldn't let them spill; she was far too angry for that. "I refuse to be a problem, waiting passively for you to solve."

He closed his eyes. "What do you want from me, Laila?" Her name croaked out of him like a protest.

She turned away. "See? You can't even say my name without sounding like you hate it."

Frustrated by her turning his attack to defence, he growled, "Will you give me a chance here? You've had months to come to terms with this. I've had barely ten minutes."

That stopped her. Her eyes searched his face, with a little puckered frown between her brows. "All right," she said slowly. "What do you want?"

"I want to make things right. I'm responsible for your life change," he replied, needing to be honest with her. "And what I don't want is for my child to think I didn't marry his mother because I didn't want him."

She jerked her arm out of his grip and lifted her chin, proud, wilful Laila Robbins to the end. "I will consider marrying you the day you can look me in the face and honestly tell me you're happy about it—that my baby and I are something more to you than messes to clean up. Not a day earlier. If I'm single—or still alive—by then," she added, with cynical smile.

"It isn't just your baby. It's mine, too." He grabbed her hand to stop her leaving, trying to ignore the sweetness of even her most reluctant touch. "This conversation would be easier if you'd think about what's best for the baby."

"You think I'm worried about me?" She turned back to stare at him, a frown between her brows. "You really don't get it. What do you think *is* best for the baby? A set of wedding rings is only best for our child if he can see the love and commitment between his parents. If he can't, he'll only blame himself for a situation he didn't create."

He dragged in a breath. She'd just described his childhood, in stark detail—the unplanned product of a brief affair turned into a quickie wedding, and the unhappy transplanting of a city girl to remote outback. And the child who'd always felt responsible every time they'd fought. If he hadn't been born…

"You keep saying 'he,'" Jake said, for the sake of something to say.

A tiny smile flitted across her face. "I know he's a boy."

He didn't argue. Jenny had been sure their child was a girl—and she'd been right.

He'd delivered the baby in their bed during a wild storm, while Jenny floated in and out of consciousness. The hospital was a five-hour drive away, the Flying Doctors couldn't land or contact him by radio, and he was all she had. That was the reality of life in the Outback: no towns or city conveniences like good roads, close schools or hospitals. Most about-to-be Outback mums moved into the nearest hospital town four weeks before the birth. He and Jenny had had the hotel booked, ready to go.

But Jenny had fallen off the chair, precipitating early labor when he was hours away, getting cattle into the trucks for sale. When he'd finally reached home, Jenny was a heap on the nursery floor, unconscious and bleeding, the storm raging overhead.

He'd tried desperately to remain focused on saving his wife and baby, but working with Jenny's blood all over his hands kept tossing his thoughts around like the freak winds outside. He watched her slipping away from him, helpless to stop it, even though he'd followed every procedure in the fully stocked medical chest the Flying Doctors gave to every isolated property in Australia.

He'd always be glad Jenny had seen Annabel once before she died. She'd been born only minutes before the Flying Doctors ran in—a minute too late for Jenny. Their tiny daughter's lungs hadn't been developed enough. She'd lived on a ventilator for five days at the Charleville Base Hospital, then quietly slipped away.

"See? You can't even smile about having a son." Laila tugged hard on his hand, until he released her. "I won't be part of a marriage that would be more like a tragedy."

He started out of his memories. Here and now he had a child on the way, and he would not let history repeat! He'd be there for Laila, for his son, every day and every night, every *hour*. "I want the baby," he said, low and intense. "I mean that."

Her laugh was short and harsh. "I can see that—but you don't want me. I get it. I got that point when you sprinted from my bed like an Olympian." She opened the stall gate. "Things have changed for me as well. I thought there was more to you than the cold loner you presented. I thought you needed a friend as well as a lover. I was wrong. Right now you couldn't pay me enough to take vows with you."

He opened his mouth, then shut it. He'd made a mull of everything he'd said to her since her fatal words *I'm pregnant*— but he couldn't acknowledge it. There was too much at risk here.

His child. This was a blessing—a *miracle* he thought he'd never have a chance to know again. No *way* was he going to let this mother and child down. He couldn't lose them.

"The life of a single parent is harder than you can imagine," he said quietly, feeling his way to what he wanted to say. Maybe a back-door approach would help—and his dad wouldn't have minded his experience being told.

The look she slanted at him was full of irony. "You might not think so, but I've been single so far by choice. Most men seem to find me attractive, and are happy to spend time with me. Baby or not, you're kidding yourself if you think I'll be single for life."

The vision flashed in his mind: pretty Laila, with all her feisty, giving sweetness, in another man's life, giving all that joy, all that life, to some other guy…

Laila, in a pool of blood, losing the baby because he wasn't there to save her—

The mere thought stabbed straight into his heart.

"You will not have this child alone, Laila," he growled. "Whether you marry me or not, I'm going to be with you from now on, day and night. I will not leave you."

She only laughed, in tired cynicism. It seemed he'd done a very thorough job of turning her off him. She didn't want to know him now.

He couldn't let it lie. No matter how noble his intentions had been before, no matter what reasons he'd had for driving her away, he refused to let her do the same. Laila was the *mother of his child*. Come drought, famine or flood, he'd be there for them both.

She was going to have to deal with the reality of him living in her face. He'd make sure this mother, this baby would *live*— but he wanted more. He would have all legal rights to his son. His child would have the Sutherland name, and all the privileges it entailed.

Even if that means going back home to Burrabilla?
Burrabilla. Where Jenny died.

He felt sick thinking about it but—could he do it, for the sake of his son's life and heritage? Could he face his wall of dark ghosts…even see Jenny's family?

Right now, he didn't know; but he felt a glow in his heart— a feeling he hadn't known for more than five long years. No matter how it came about, he was going to be a daddy.

There was no way he'd take that miracle for granted this time. He'd make sure Laila was safe, that the baby came into the world safe and at the right time—and he was going to be a daily part of his child's life, no matter what. He wanted to be there to read bedtime stories, to see their first step, their first tooth…to hear those first, lisping words. No way would he handle being an every-second-weekend dad—and his child shouldn't have to put up with second best. He owed his child that.

It all came down to Laila. He had to find a way to make her marry him; but so far his words were only alienating her.

Yet he'd won her over the night they'd made love, without saying a word…so maybe he should put his mouth to a better use—one Laila seemed to appreciate a few months ago.

CHAPTER THREE

THE look on his face alerted Laila, just as he leaned in. He wanted to seduce her into accepting his proposal—and she was terrified he'd win.

She hated him…at least, she wanted to hate him…but she was horribly afraid she didn't. Could the fascination still blast her from her feet, and her certainty that marriage to a man who didn't love them both would ruin her life—and the baby's?

She had to resist the look in his eyes as he leaned toward her, his burning-hot gaze fixed on her mouth. And she would resist, in a moment…

Next thing she knew she was lying on the hay, not knowing whether she was escaping his touch or surrendering to it—and she didn't know if she cared. Jake leaned into her, with a glow of satisfaction in eyes now dark gold. With the tiniest curve of his mouth, not enough to be a smile—more like a look of triumph—that incredible mouth came down on hers.

Desperate to fight him, she pushed on his chest to get up, like he was a fence or a wall she could use; but with the tiniest touch of his finger under her chin, her lips parted, wanting, needing the kiss she relived in her bed every night. With the lightest movement of his lips on hers, she moaned, her arms wrapping around his neck, pulling him down to her. Oh, the joy of having him close, having his warmth, his hands and mouth touching her again, making her feel so feminine, so alive, after months of wondering if she'd ever find a way.

He moved over her, one hand caressing her cheek and throat, the other tangled in her hair. His mouth was light, clinging, exquisite in unexpected tenderness—

Without any of the despairing need he'd been driven by the first time.

If there was only one thing she knew about Jake, it was the desire to live she'd felt burning just beneath the surface of the rigid control he projected. He always seemed to refuse to give in to that need—but then it had burst to life the last time he'd touched her.

It wasn't there now. The rigid control she hated had taken its place; he gave only to her, accepting no passion or tenderness in return.

Much as she longed to, she couldn't fool herself into thinking this meant he'd developed feelings for her. She was the means to getting the one thing he *did* want.

Though she yearned for nothing more than to lose reality in the drifting passion he'd engendered in her, she forced herself to move. She pushed him off hard enough to make him fall back into the hay. She jumped to her feet, staring down at him. "You hypocrite, using me to get what you want. Well, here's a news flash for you—I don't need this. I don't need you." She got to her feet and stared down at him with all the contempt she could muster.

After a moment, he followed her to his feet. "You're right. The last thing you might need is a man like me in your life— but you should have thought of that before the night of the party. You're stuck with me now. You're the mother of my child. I will be his father, Laila, whether you like it or not— whether you like me or not," he said, his full, sensual mouth turned down.

The grim words snapped her out of her fury. He was staring down into her face, in the soft, unfocused light that marked the beginning of sunset—but even in the gentle gloom, she could see the blazing self-hate in those amazing amber-gold depths, making her rethink the little she knew about this enigma of a man.

"I never said you couldn't be his father, Jake. You can see him whenever you want —"

"No." The word was harsh, uncompromising. "I won't be a second-weekend, come-for-school-concerts or visit-for-dinner dad. I will be his father day and night. *Every* day and night."

Shocked, she stared at him. This level of commitment was the last thing she'd expected. "It won't happen."

He looked into her eyes, dark, blazing, intense. "It will. That's a promise. If you don't marry me, I'll move in next door to wherever you go, or across the street. I will be there for you—and for my child."

He said he'd be there for me as well as the baby. He put me first...

Her rebel mind briefly wondered how he'd look if he ever smiled; and by natural progression, the memory came. She'd never forget how exquisite it felt to have that beautiful mouth locked against hers in the white-hot depths of passion—the passion she'd only glimpsed in those dead-and-blazing-alive eyes that night.

Would she ever know such passion again?

"You may not like me, but I swear to you now, Laila, by all I hold sacred, that I won't let my child down. I won't let you down again."

The passion in his vow scattered her thoughts, and sent her focus straight back to the here and now; because some deep instinct told her that he meant every word.

She squeezed her eyes shut. She'd thought he'd cut and run as he had the night after they'd made love, but he'd just made a solemn vow to stand by her—

Oh, how she hated the weakness! With a touch, a kind word,

he could make her feel so tempted to accept that broad shoulder to lean on, to know that if she married him, at least she wouldn't be smothered by a man who loved her too much—

Or at all. He only wants the baby. I'd be married to a man who wouldn't give me the love I need, but who wouldn't let me go.

She felt every Robbins forebear, tough and unyielding as the land they lived and died on, ranging behind her back as she fought him—and her own weakness. She would not accept less than the life and love she needed…that their baby would need.

"I don't see why we're complicating this," she said with a casual air she prayed wasn't overdone. "You needed to know about the baby, so I told you. I don't need to be protected or supported. Maybe I could get back to my life in Bathurst by next term, and ask for late exams. You stay here on the land, doing your thing. I'll call you when you're a daddy."

Silence fell on them like the shimmering waves of late-afternoon, almost-summer heat surrounding the warm barn. The quiet was tense, anxious. The anticipation sat on her like the aura of dry heat everywhere. Unable to stand it, she opened her eyes.

Jake just stared at her, as if she'd said something profound, or stunning.

"You don't need to worry about me," she insisted, feeling as if Jake were waiting for the rest of what she had to say. "Go on with your work. I'll be fine on my own."

Then, with shocking suddenness, the unease shattered with the sound of hard-edged laughter. Jake was holding his sides with the gusts of uncontrollable mirth—but it wasn't a happy sound. "Oh, that's good," he gasped. "That's just precious. The perfect irony." He kept laughing, oblivious to her reaction. "So God has a sense of humor, after all."

She'd wanted to know how he looked when he smiled—but this felt too poignant, too sad. He wasn't laughing—it was too cynical and self-hating for that—and it made her heart bleed for him. What had happened to this man?

She had to harden her heart to force the words out. "What did I say that was so funny?"

He shook his head as if clearing it, as if just remembering she was there. The laughter died from his face before he gave a soft, muffled curse. "It wasn't you—it's the warped full circle coming back to complete the circus that's my life."

He didn't volunteer anything more, and she knew he wouldn't. His self-hate had obviously been a party of one for a long time, and he wouldn't let anyone else in the door. But he refused to walk out on his child.

How could that kind of marriage ever be the right thing? After seeing Dar and Marcie's happiness, and seeing Danni make any guy interested in her jump through hoops to just get a date, she knew two things: she wouldn't take less than the best and she wouldn't allow her baby to grow up with less than complete love and total security.

Better to have two parents who both adored him but lived apart than to allow her child to endure a childhood like Danni's.

"I'm sorry, but this whole situation makes no sense." She spoke with all the bluntness in her nature. "You can live in a separate house from us, and our child will still know you love him—all you need do is visit or take him for a night, or school breaks. I swear to you I won't ever block your rights to him."

"It's not enough." His whole attention seemed absorbed in watching his thumb flicking in and out of a hand curled into a fist.

"Why? Why are you pushing for all of this?" she asked, wondering how he made even such a small thing as moving a finger so enthralling; she couldn't move her gaze from him. "I'm not under any illusions. I could have been any woman that night. You barely knew who I was. You know you don't need to support me financially. You could walk and no one would blame you—"

"You're wrong."

She frowned. "No need to be chivalrous about it. Being a single parent really isn't that big a deal these days—"

The intensity of his hooded gaze stopped her words. "I knew it was you that night. All night, I knew it was you."

The heat from his eyes, the force in those stark words, hit her over and over. It zinged between them, a cloud of everything he'd left unspoken…and the woman in her, ripened with the hormones of pregnancy, melting with memory of their one bittersweet night, and on high alert since the kiss they'd shared—ached with wanting. He hadn't wanted just any woman that night, he'd wanted *her*. "Then why did you leave me like that?" she whispered.

His gaze burned on her a moment longer, before he turned away with startling abruptness. "I had my reasons." Knife-edged as the land outside in its harshness, his voice tore into her hopes and fears with a serrated edge.

Four simple words, yet they were another door shutting in her face.

But no matter how he tried to make her believe otherwise, he did want her. It wasn't the heat, or the promise in his eyes as he'd said it; nothing so cliché, or so simple. No, it was history repeating, in a few intense words. The stark need in his voice, the ache inside his eyes told its story…and the heavy ripeness in the air between them. His desire for her hadn't changed—even if he'd die rather than admit it.

Another notch of violet darkness fell inside the barn, as if it were digitalized. Something inside Laila shifted, moving the romantic blinders from her eyes, revealing questions she'd barely known were there: the doubts had been there all along. *You still want me, so why can't this be real? What are you hiding from?*

As if he'd heard her silent questions, his jaw set. With the slanted line of cheekbone, hair like midnight, and strange, intense eyes that changed hue with every play of light and shadow, he seemed like a flint carving: cold, remote—and too compelling to walk away from.

His voice, when it broke into her reverie, was flat and grim, without the dark, smoky music that haunted her dreams. "I still have my reasons, Laila."

Yet his gaze stayed on her mouth for a moment before lifting to her eyes; they were still lush and uncompromising at once, still *needing*. His hands curled into fists, as if he was making a physical effort not to touch her.

Maybe he was…

If his reasons for not wanting a relationship with her were so strong that he'd lie to her about wanting her, turn from her, act as if he didn't like her or even *see* her—and even now, to offer her a marriage in name only, though he was aching as badly for her as she was for him—

Then that made all the difference in the world. He wanted her, needed her even; but something made him feel as if he couldn't give in to that craving.

She might not know why…but she wasn't going to allow the status quo to remain. She had more aces in her deck than she'd known about only an hour ago.

Testing the waters, she said softly, "Do you really think we could have a platonic marriage, after we've already been lovers?"

He frowned, and moved back through the gate. "Yes. It won't happen again."

He was backing off…and she wanted to shout, to laugh and twirl around—because his rigid control had slipped with the power of one question.

Next ace, please…

She moved toward him, slow and gentle, still wearing a half smile. "Who are you trying to fool with your lies, you or me?"

Jake's nostrils flared, sensing her change from anger and defensiveness to tender aggression…using that soft, luscious smile she used when she felt hopeful. The sweet ripeness of a woman who now knew she was wanted by the man she desired.

He'd always known he wouldn't have gone anywhere with another woman the night of the Robbins's anniversary party. It was Laila, *only* Laila who tempted him right out of his self-control and made him a man again. She'd been driving him crazy from her first smile, and with the look in those laughing eyes that told him she knew he wasn't the human island he tried to be.

And now she'd found the chink in his armor—she knew he wanted her. If he let her open the crack any wider, she'd give him her loving body, snuggle right down inside his heart, and want to know about his life, see his home—

Home. Where his wife's blood was on his hands.

No—*no*! He'd thought he could do it if he had to—that maybe he'd moved on enough—but now he knew he couldn't go back…not even for the sake of this new child. No matter how much he wanted it, *ached* to go home, with every fiber of his being.

He didn't deserve to go home—or to have the chance of happiness Laila held out to him.

"You're the one who's the fool," he snapped, desperate to close his armor back over. "Just because I wanted you for one night doesn't mean it will happen again."

Her smile only grew. "You're a liar," she said softly, taking another step toward him. "Prove it, Connors."

Now he really wanted to bolt. The softer, more feminine she became the weaker he became around her—a man again, with a man's most basic needs denied for far too long. She'd ripped his delusion of control by seeing through his attempt to seduce her into marriage.

When she wasn't insecure, it was as if she could see right through him…and now she was the enchanting, wise woman-child who'd snared his mind and taken control of his body from the first day, she was locking into his every hormone with the instincts of a heat-seeking missile.

He wanted her like crazy; she wanted him like crazy. Neither of them could hide it. One touch now and the need would explode.

"That's the deal," he grated, hoping he didn't sound as crazy with hunger as he felt. "I'll act like I'm in love with you in front of your family, if you want. I'll give you a home and security and you can go back once the baby's born to finish your degree. I'll get a different job, one that lets me work my schedule around yours to mind the baby when it comes. I'll do whatever it takes to make your life right, but there's no promise of love and more babies."

And that would never change. Love in the Australian Outback was as risky as a walk across the Sahara without a water bottle. The Outback had a remoteness as old as time, far from the modern life most people knew. An emptiness that could be deadly, for it killed without conscience or pity, destroying families, taking lives before they'd even begun.

Watching Jenny and his baby girl Annabel die right before his eyes had burned that lesson into his brain with a branding iron. Marriages rarely survived out here unless both parties were committed to the life, like Brian and Marcie.

Laila loved it out here, he had no doubt of that—but that was only during vacation. She loved living in Bathurst, too; she'd told him that. Bathurst was in the country, sure, hours west of Sydney—but it was a small city, with plenty of restaurants, banks, schools and safe roads, and most importantly, a fine hospital. It was a far cry from the reality of the remote life here.

His body turned to ice, cooling his ardor.

"I'm taking you back to Bathurst next week," he said abruptly. "Ask for a late exam. I'll support you. I'll find another job, or buy a farm close to all amenities."

She gasped. "You can *afford* to buy a farm? Bathurst's far from cheap."

He nodded in silence.

Her gaze on him was narrow, assessing. "I gather you're still working on the assumption that I'll marry you?"

He shrugged, half turning toward the outside of the barn. The last of the day's light had painted the barn door a violent magenta. He wondered why none of the guys had stomped in to dump their tools or to check on him; but he was glad they hadn't. He needed to feel more in control—to make Laila lose that tender, confident sensuality.

"At this point I don't care if we're married or not." He kept his voice hard. "I offered that for your sake, and your family. But where you and my child go, I'm going to be, with or without a ring and licence. If you decide to stay at your apartment, I'll move in next door. I can live in the city—I did it for five years, though I prefer living on the land."

About to snap back at him, Laila realized he was trying to alienate her again, to keep her off balance—and to make her forget her questions. She was rattling his cage—and by heaven, she'd keep at it, until he gave in. "You lived in the city?"

"A city." He didn't add to that; she hadn't expected him to confirm which city it had been. "I didn't like it much."

But he was willing to return to that life, for the sake of her education, and for their child.

He'd seemed the stuff heroes were made of since she'd first seen him—now she knew that he was. He loved the Outback, but would return to the city for her sake. He wanted her like crazy, and had done his level best to keep his distance from her. He offered her marriage, knowing it would be little less than sexual torture for them both, because he believed it was the right and honorable thing to do—for her, as well as the child. Anyone who knew Dar would know how sick with disappointment he'd be if she came to him pregnant and alone...

I'm the last thing you need.

Yes, she knew exactly what Jake Connors was: a self-hating, tortured white knight willing to sacrifice his wants and needs so she could keep her dreams alive.

The day headed toward night. The workers would break their solitude any minute now, putting their gear in the tack room before heading to the mess for dinner.

She walked into the stall next to her beloved Starfire to groom the next horse, ignoring the gelding's restless sidestepping. Lightning was well-known for his feisty nature, even after he'd been gelded.

Jake stood silent, watching her. Waiting. Well, she was too tired right now to volunteer information—at least until he started giving part of himself in return.

She was a third of the way through before she asked the question burning her brain. "So is your idea of marrying me, or moving to Bathurst to be near the baby and me, some part of a grand plan? Are you trying to redeem yourself for your past sins?"

"You got it." Jake's laugh was short and bitter as he joined her, picking up another currycomb. "The universal slate-wiper will make my sins disappear if I do the right thing by a pregnant girl with every other means of care at her disposal. The world works that way, right?" He bent under Lightning's flanks, combing his belly, and the horse stopped his edgy dance. "It's not the world's forgiveness I care about. I don't believe in karma."

She flinched at his whiplash tone, even though he aimed it at himself. "What do you believe in, then?"

He twisted his face to glance at her, his eyes dull, like old gold encased in an unlit case. "What did you believe in before your life fell apart, Princess Laila? Why is everyone wrong about you?"

He didn't expect her to answer. He'd already shut the door to his world in her face, guarding it with a solid wall of icy politeness.

His nerves on sudden high alert, Lightning shied, sidestepping her next combing. Moments later, a distant rumble of thunder reached them: another dry storm was on its way.

"You should go into the house. It's going to be dangerous here soon." His tone was remote. It seemed, as far as he was concerned, the discussion was over.

The thuds of booted feet came toward them. A voice called from outside the tack room door, "Hey, Jake, it's comin' up for dinnertime if you're in here."

With a quick motion, Jake tossed the currycomb into the feed stall and grabbed Laila, walking her backward until they reached the close wall that blocked them from view.

His body, taut and summer-hot, was flush against hers, holding her with every part of him; she inhaled his outdoor and male scent, could taste it if she just went up on her tiptoes...

"What are you doing?" she whispered.

"Maintaining our privacy until you've made a decision." He looked down at her, that old, rigid control in his eyes—the control that no longer fooled her. "They won't come looking for me. They let me keep to myself."

"I've already made my—"

"Laila, you in here?" That was the voice of Laila's brother Glenn.

With a tiny, exasperated sound, Jake covered her mouth with his finger. He whispered fiercely in her ear, "If they find us together, the news will reach your dad in minutes. Are you ready to tell him our news?"

At this moment she wasn't ready for anything but to make that finger against her lips turn into his mouth, to wrap her arms around him, to take more than a one-night taste of him...

Not knowing what else to do, she shook her head. Unconsciously her body moved against his, and with a tiny groan, he lowered his head to hers—

A loud bark of laughter from one of the men made them

jump, and move apart. The voices faded to silence, but their work was done. Jake kept looking down at her, his face tight with emotion he was holding in check.

"We should go, before Dar or the boys come looking for me," she said quietly. "We both know they will in the next few minutes if I don't answer their call."

Jake opened the stall gate for her. He locked it behind them once they'd walked through. Lightning wasn't a horse to remain passively in his stall with a storm around.

Clouds were chasing each other around a darkening sky, with trailing shreds of the riotous display of color that was a common Outback sunset. Laila drew in a cleansing breath of the hard-hitting wind tossing her hair about her face. It had been hot and still here for too many weeks—as stagnant as her life had been for too many years.

"When you're ready to face your parents, I'll be there with you," was the only thing he said as they headed up the gentle incline toward the main house.

"All right, but—"

"Don't say I don't have to. I want to do this." His voice was fierce.

"All right," she said again, knowing he had made the best choice; her father would respect him for standing beside her. "They deserve to know who the father is, and what I intend to do in the future."

"What *we* intend." His voice was inflexible.

"I guess we'll inform them of that when we come to a consensus on what that entails." She hoped her lack of argument would confuse and frustrate him.

"I'll leave you here," he said as they reached the tall fence separating the main house from the rest of the property. He turned to go.

She couldn't let him go, not like this, with so much left unspoken; but the first words that came to her were a continuation of what she was saying before. "You might have lived there, but you couldn't be a city fella. Jackarooing isn't a job any average Joe can do. You need experience and skill to mend the fences properly, to round up the sheep or to ride as you do—and no one could doubt your skill. You're living poetry on a horse." Like those long-haired, wild-hearted horseback warriors she'd always fantasized about as a girl.

He looked over his shoulder at her, unexpectedly grinning at her comment. His smile lit up those amazing eyes of his, and her rebel-fool heart did that fluttery flip again. "I was born and bred in the Outback. I spent five years in the city, but I came back fourteen years ago."

Startled, she asked, "How old are you? You don't look a day older than thirty."

He lifted a brow as his grin grew. "Thanks—I think. But I'll be forty in two years. My mother's genetics—her mother's Asian, and both my mother and grandmother look young. Dad looked almost twice her age. Aaron, Sandy and I all inherited my mother's looks."

Laila heard and registered the name—Aaron must be his brother, and Sandy, his sister—and she even recognized the reasons behind Jake's saying anything personal: he was trying to get close to her. But all she could think was, *he looks amazing when he smiles.* The just-crooked grin brought his amber and gold eyes to life, showed up a dimple in his left cheek and made him irresistible, even more so than when he was dark and with-drawn.

And finally, his belief that she was a child fell into place, as did his willingness to take full responsibility for her pregnancy. He was a man, with all a man's maturity.

"Is your mother still alive?" she asked, hearing his use of *looked* in relation to his father.

"Yes." The word was blunt, stark. He offered no more.

"Are you older or younger than your sister and brother?"

"Four years older. They're twins." Now his voice was taut, tense with aching, like a cow rope fraying. "It's been just the three of us—Sandy, Aaron and me, for a long time."

"How long?" she asked softly. Wondering why his mother wasn't in the family picture, or his grandmother.

"Years." The words were a door closing in her face. "I'd better go for dinner. The guys will come looking for me if I miss it." Another wry smile. "A guy can miss a lot of things, but not food or beer, or the footy on TV. The guys won't stand for that."

Obviously he felt he'd told her enough for one day; but at least now he was talking, not just speaking words. He was communicating. This was the man she'd glimpsed before.

"Good night," she said dully, feeling as if the life in her world was leaving her. Back to the polite evasions that had been her lot since coming back home. At least with Jake she had no need to pretend.

"We'll talk tomorrow," he called back, heading down the hill.

Without warning she burst out, "What is there to say? Haven't we said enough?"

"There's plenty to say." He turned back and moved to her, his face fierce, his skin glowing in the stormy half-light. "Like where we're going to live, what doctor you're seeing, how we make a living. We have to make plans."

"You don't get it, do you?" she snapped, with a weariness born of her world turning on its axis in a single day. "I said no."

"I heard." He was right in front of her now, his hands on her shoulders. "But you don't seem to get one fundamental fact. I will make sure you and the baby are safe and well for the rest of your lives. They're the facts, Laila."

Dear God, the man was beautiful…and he scrambled her wits every time he touched her. She had to pull herself together, or he'd take full control of her life…

"What about what I want?" she asked desperately. "Or doesn't that matter?"

One hand left her shoulder to touch her chin. "Tell me, Laila," he said softly, moving closer still. "Tell me what you want."

The wind turned softer, and moved between them like a warm current of wanting. *Want, want...he said want, didn't he? He asked what I want...*

How to say, *I just want you to love me*, without making a total fool of herself again?

"I want what every woman wants," she said in little more than a whisper, knowing her face, her body, must be reflecting the aching inside her: the yearning for him to touch her. "A few kids. A nice place—maybe a farm with a clinic attached—for my practice." And before she knew it, she was blurting out the truth. "No—that's not what I really want. Those things would be lovely—but they're not necessary. I can do without almost everything else, but I have to be loved. I want my husband to love me, with all his heart."

The wind had died moments before. The air around them was dull and hot. Another quick rumbling sound came from the southwest. A crack of thunder hit a field to the south of the house.

With a muffled curse he dropped his hands. His face was as white as his golden skin would allow, his eyes burning. "They're nice dreams, Laila. I wish I could give them to you, but I can't." He strode away from her as if chased by a fury of demons.

He would never love her.

She watched him go, aching and hurting for a man she wanted like crazy but barely knew. She'd only scratched the surface of what haunted him, and what she knew didn't tally.

A man willing to give up his life for her sake and her baby's, but who expected nothing for himself—not even normal relations between husband and wife.

A man with all the reticent pride of his forebears, yet humble to the point of self-hatred.

He was rich enough to buy a farm in Bathurst, but he worked as a simple jackaroo and lived in a communal quarters with twenty other guys.

His eyes turned to molten gold when he looked at her, his body grew hard when she was near him, but he constantly did all he could to push her away.

His voice grew thick with love as he spoke of his family, yet he'd never left Wallaby Station in the year he'd been here.

Who was the real Jake Connors?

Somewhere in his terse, unvarnished story lay the whole truth. He'd tossed her only a few jagged pieces today—pieces hard and sharp enough for her to cut the remains of her sensual daydreams of him into bloodied shreds.

But it hadn't worked. Something inside her told her that nothing designed to turn her away from Jake would ever work. Even if she married a nice, average guy, got the house and kids and a picket fence around her vet practice, she'd remain utterly fascinated by, and helplessly drawn to Jake Connors until the day she died.

She couldn't let him leave, not when she knew she'd spend every day of the next fifty years waiting, hoping he'd come to her so she could see him one more time, just as she'd done every day and night of the past year…

"Jake!" she cried, bolting into the thick, warm evening, heavy with fast-moving gray clouds: the promise of rain that never seemed to fall, and wouldn't fall tonight. "Jake! *Jake!*"

He'd almost reached the men's quarters, the old shearers' rooms painted and remodeled with the most basic of comforts, and a communal TV/games room. He halted when she cried his name, but he didn't turn around, didn't speak. Waiting.

A fork of lightning split the velvet-purple sky with shreds of turbulent cloud, landing with a violent crack somewhere behind the century-old, tumbledown shearers' huts. With a long, tearing sound, a branch fell to earth.

Jake seemed to be part of the earth and night and sky—even the night storm. Stark and hot, he was a man beautiful beyond her every dream or imagining, untamed and untamable.

What arrogance or stupidity had made her believe a man like Jake could ever be hers? He was as far out of her reach as a comet, too fast and too high for a mortal like her to grasp; but like an obsessed astronomer, she kept gazing upward at what she could never have or hold.

Dumbstruck, awestruck, rapt and terrified, Laila stared, trying to form words, but none came to her clumsy mouth.

"What is it?" He didn't turn. His voice was curt, as tight as his body.

She couldn't remember; the need was back, the terrible, wonderful ache that always filled her when she was near him. Poles apart they might be, but north was heading south at warp speed, and even with all she thought she knew about him, she couldn't do a thing to stop it.

One step, two, and then she was running, stumbling to him, her rebel mouth rasping his name with all the anguished craving he inspired in her. His past and his rejections didn't matter, not now, when the waves of need hitting her were coming back as strongly from him.

She'd never hold him for long; but right now the coming heartache didn't matter, either. As he had that first night, he needed her tonight, and that was enough. She'd make it be enough. She cannoned into his body, and wrapped her arms around his stone-hard form from behind.

"I was wrong," she whispered into his taut back, reveling in the touch, the heat searing her even through his rough clothes. "I don't want average."

His voice was like a saw across hardwood, cutting them both. "Your dreams will die with me, Laila. You'll regret this—

maybe not tomorrow, next week or next year—but one day, you'll wish you'd never met me. Please, just take what I'm offering and stop wanting more." His voice was gravel-sharp, and just as unbending. "I know you want more—and I'll only hurt you."

"I know," she said hopelessly. "But you've put a padlock on my soul, and I can't take it off. I'm bound to you, Jake. I don't know why," she cried softly. "I don't want to be, but one look at you and I'm gone."

"Gone." He gave one of those awful, mirthless laughs that pierced her heart. "That's a good term for the effect I have on people. They're gone—or they wish I was, before long."

"Stop it," she cried fiercely. "You won't push me away, not tonight."

He turned in her arms, and tipped up her face with a finger: the only connection he would give, but it streaked through her with the searing, melting heat of a bushfire. "You'll regret it."

"Maybe I will," she admitted, "but right now all I think about is you, all I want is you."

He held her off, and wouldn't touch her, or hold her—but the look in his eyes was molten with need, just as it had been the night they'd made love...

So she moved into his body, becoming the aggressor.

"Just give me now, Jake," she mumbled between the kisses he miraculously wasn't stopping. Oh, thank you, *thank you God*, he was lifting his throat, drinking in her kisses; the low growls weren't from a man in the grip of tortured rejection, but the darkest of pleasure...

His hands were a bare half-inch from her skin, and at the feel of the radiant heat coming from inside him, her body pounded out a primitive tattoo from deep inside her, sending out the subtle, drenched scent of a woman who wants a man. *Touch me, Jake, touch me...*

Another fork of lightning clove the heat of the night in two, tearing it down with an earsplitting dry crack. But Laila wouldn't even have noticed had its electrifying light not brought his face to vivid, stark life. Jake suddenly became living flesh, all fierce, savage male, a man wired on a knife's edge—and the flashpoint of heat in his eyes told her that he'd seen, felt, taken in the scent of her need. Man to woman, basic and primal.

Finally, oh, at last he stopped fighting it, hauled her up hard against him and kissed her.

CHAPTER FOUR

LAILA STAGGERED back under the raw power he unleashed on her—dear God, the man could kiss when he lost control.

Glorious insanity, insatiable hunger, a blaze burning all it touched in high, raging winds—it was all that and more. He kissed her as if he wanted to eat her alive, and she was devouring him in return, mouth-to-mouth.

It had been like this last time—this uncontrollable, unstoppable, *perfect* passion. It was everything she'd read about and dreamed of, but had never known with any man until Jake.

He couldn't hide it now, and didn't try. The kiss was drugging her with its intensity, with the raw male need coming from him, bringing her long-hidden femininity to glorious life. She moaned and arched her ripening body against his, hearing his growl of satisfaction with a rippling thrill. He pulled her even closer, his hands all over her, leaving her alive and aching and filled with blazing heat, wanting more...

Muted laughter came from the big, barnlike structure used as a communal dining room. A voice floated toward where they held and touched each other, challenging someone else to a game of pool.

Jake tore his mouth from hers; and, weak and limp and shocked, burned alive by the depths of her fire when he touched her, Laila let her head fall to his shoulder.

"Go," he grated. "Go home where you're safe, before we do something you'll regret."

At that, her head snapped back up, and she laughed, because he meant it. "How can it damage me any further, Jake? The horse has already bolted. I'm pregnant." She heard the unsteady tone in her voice, but didn't care. After that kiss, she couldn't be sure of anything except that her knees had given way, her body was hollow with pain-filled need, and she was more gloriously alive than she'd ever been.

"This isn't part of the deal." He pushed himself back from her, but keeping his hands at her waist to be sure she didn't fall. Protecting her even when she threw that offer back in his face. "I'm giving you my name. My protection. That's all."

She gaped for a moment before she let out another peal of laughter: a sound tinged with hysteria. "You almost made love to me standing up against a wall, and you're still offering only a marriage of convenience?"

For once, he was in the light and she was in shadow. By the soft beams of a slow-rising moon and the wild cracks of lightning now moving north, she saw his jaw harden, chiseled in the granite of his innate stubbornness. "It won't happen again. I won't let it happen again."

She kept laughing, but it was weaker now, tired. "That's it, keep lying to yourself. Maybe, eventually, I'll believe it, too."

His nostrils flared, and she knew she'd pushed him too far. "That's all I'm willing to give. I'll act like I'm crazy about you for your family's sake. I'll give you a home and security and you can finish your degree. I'll work my schedule around yours to mind the baby when it comes. I'll do whatever it takes to make your life right—you deserve all that, and more—but I won't make love to you. You either agree to that now, or I pack my things and leave Wallaby tonight, and you go in there and face your family alone, with the truth."

A chill snaked through her at the thought, because she knew

he'd do it. *Fool!* She'd pushed him too far. He wasn't ready to hear the truth of what they could be, or even what he wanted. So typical of her to want it all, and to do whatever it took to get it now.

Would she never learn to wait?

She'd never been a coward, but to face her family with the truth—to see all her family's pride in her achievements, and their rainbow-shaded illusions about her, shatter in an instant…

"All right," she said quietly. She felt vulnerable and emotional, and, apart from disappearing, having her baby elsewhere and giving it up for adoption, Jake had given her the only way out she could consider taking.

"All right? That's it?" His gaze narrowed on her, as if searching for a legal loophole in her simple words, but Laila kept her expression meek, without challenge.

"That's it," she answered, wondering to herself if he'd even noticed that his hands were no longer just holding her up, but were caressing her waist and hips, keeping that slow melt inside her alive, pooling the heat, stoking the fire.

"You'll marry me?" he asked, his gaze dark and intent on hers.

She drew in a breath. "No. I accept that what you say is true for you. And I ask for you to accept that to me, that's completely inadequate. I don't know who you are, where you come from or what you want in life—and what you're offering under the circumstances is nowhere near enough, not for me. I won't marry a martyr. I will accept your role in life with our child, and an acknowledgment of paternity for my family—but that's all."

The silence was absolute. He didn't move, but in the light of a wild cracking fork of lightning, she saw the moment his face changed: the vulnerability he'd hidden from the world shone through. Despite his assertions, maybe deep down in his heart, where he didn't dare to look, or acknowledge his desires, he *did* want something more…

He leaned a clenched fist against the wall of the communal room, his breathing uneven. The touch of some deeper emotion at her rejection—dare she call it devastation?—in his eyes resonated in her heart, making him want to take it all back, and say yes, she'd marry him, give him this baby, anything to make him feel safe and happy again.

"I'll let you know when I'm ready to tell my family," she said, fighting to keep her voice—and her resolve—steady.

He looked at her, the anguish not yet under control—and her rebel heart ached and burned to say the words that would make him smile. But she couldn't risk the ultimate happiness of all three of them. To be a true family—to have that wonderful joy of a loving family—she had to fight. She would accept nothing less.

"I will change your mind, Laila." His voice was rough velvet.

A shiver ran up her spine in response, as she wondered just how many times she could make him try to change her mind by means of those addicting kisses and rough, sensual touch. Jake was like the land they both loved: hot, unbending, with sudden, total changes in nature, and sometimes cruel in its savagery—but like the land, she couldn't walk from him. There was so much more to Jake Connors than he showed to the world. "Maybe I'll change yours instead," she said softly. "Every time you're working on bringing me around to your point of view, Jake Connors, I'll be working on making you want what I want. Take that as a warning. I want happiness…and I won't take anything less."

If anything, his face grew even darker. Without a word, he pushed off the wall, turned, and walked into the communal room.

Well, she'd thrown down the gauntlet. The challenge was on—and given that she knew now how badly he wanted her, she hoped she knew where to place her bets.

From alone and terrified, within a few hours, she'd found a

few unexpected aces inside her sleeve. He honestly believed this marriage he wanted would be a passionless arrangement, a marriage in name only to give her baby a name and a father— but she wanted him and he wanted her, and it was going to happen. The passion hovering in the air between them, like the lightning cracking from the dry clouds above, would explode one day, and soon.

He might not think he deserved anything good from this crazy, selfless offer, but she was going to show him just how much he deserved.

There was so much about him she didn't know, including what had happened to him to make him the intense, withdrawn man she knew had once been foreign to his nature. She would find the whole truth, would come to know the man inside this fascinating enigma. She'd make him want to be her lover, as well as a father for their baby.

She smiled, but it soon faded at the thought of the real, monu-mental task before her: telling the family. Could she face them with the cover story Jake had hinted at? She hadn't lied to them since childhood escapades, and over something so important—

For their sakes, for their affectionate illusions of her, she had to try.

I can't do it.

She'd almost convinced herself it was the right thing to pretend she and Jake were in love, to protect them from the consequences of her stupidity. But faced with the loving, anxious faces surrounding her—the men who'd dedicated their lives to protecting her, and the woman who'd given her mother-love and freedom—Laila couldn't go through with the lines she had rehearsed the past two weeks.

If she gave them the cover story, not only would she wind up hurting them more later when they knew the truth, but she knew she'd wind up married to Jake within a week.

She glanced at Jake—and suddenly, the thought of being the wife of a man who claimed he could never love her sent exploding pain through her chest. While it would help her now, the reality of her life would be intolerable, *unbearable*. She had been kidding herself. How could she live with a man who barely even liked her? He might want her, but it wasn't as if she had a lot of competition out here.

She was having his child but didn't even know him well enough to be sure if he'd wanted her in truth, or because he was a man and there were no other candidates to take care of his needs. She didn't know him at all, because he didn't let her in—and she couldn't bear to be forever standing by him, waiting just outside the barricaded doors of his heart, aching for what would never happen.

I'm sorry, Dar, Marcie…I just can't go through with this, even for your sakes.

Jake had never met such a hardheaded, stubborn woman in all his days.

Facing her father, stepmother and brothers with the news, Jake fumed in silence. He'd expected her to come around to his plans within a week or two. He'd banked on what he knew: Laila wasn't the kind of person to blithely tell her conservative and overprotective family that she was about to become a single mother—

But that's what she'd just done.

She hadn't exactly been blithe about it, but if she was anxious, she was hiding it well. She'd just sat down beside her father in the living room where she'd called the family conference, took his hand, and said, "I know you're worried about me. I'm sorry for that. I need to tell you all what's been going on."

Glenn, the more blunt-spoken of her brothers—the most like her—frowned, looking at him, Jake. "What's *he* doing here?"

Brian said quietly, "I have a feeling he's involved in the

problem…right, Laila?" The soft tones in no way hid the grimness within. His gaze speared Jake like twin laser sights.

Laila said softly, "You know, don't you, Dar?"

His gaze still on Jake, Brian nodded. The look was hard and unrelenting. "Marcie said you'd tell us in your time. Or maybe it was in his time." He jerked his head toward Jake.

Laila's smile was faint. "You should know me better than that, Dar. When did I ever do anything in someone else's time or way?"

"Well, if it was ever in my time or way, Princess, I missed the moment."

Seeing the hurt flash in Laila's eyes, Jake found himself wanting to jump in and defend her—but he was the outsider here, and he had a feeling Laila needed to do this alone; but for a self-contained man, keeping his mouth shut had never been a harder task.

"But that's the trouble, Dar." Laila's voice was soft, sad, yet definite. "I might have fought it, but life has always been *your* time, *your* way. I might not have gone to *your* university or chose the course you wanted me to do, but it doesn't matter. Everyone knows who I am—or, more to the point, who *you* are. Your wings are always over me—overshadowing me." She looked around Brian to Marcie, who was sitting in silence on her husband's other side, willing her stepmother to support her. "No matter what I do, you define me. People see me as the great Brian Robbins's daughter. Nothing that I can say or do seems to change it." She cocked her head over toward Jake. "Even he believes it. Especially him."

Identical hurt, flash for flash, father to daughter—and then reluctant understanding came into Brian's eyes. "So you got pregnant to change your image, to escape my shadow? Did you have to prove to him who you are in such a personal way?"

The rough tones were full of too much pain for Jake to take offence at Brian's reasons why Laila had come to him that night.

Laila's brothers both made identical growling sounds, and glared at Jake.

"You know better than that, too." Laila sighed. "If it was about escaping, or establishing my identity, all I had to do was to finish my course and start a veterinary practice far away from here or the Ghost Gum estate. That would have hurt you enough—but I never wanted to hurt you. I just wanted to find a way to live my life, my way—and on the way I made a mistake. The pregnancy was unplanned."

Andrew and Glenn sucked in collective breaths as they continued to glare at Jake. "So when are you going to marry her?" Andrew's normally friendly tones were Arctic.

Glenn had his fists curled. "Soon enough." He took a striding step forward.

Brian nodded. "It will need to happen soon." His gaze fell to Laila's gently rounded tummy. "She'll be showing properly in a week or two—though that won't stop the talk."

Looking tired and emotional, Marcie sighed, and seemed about to mediate the escalating male passions—but it was Laila's next words that gained everyone's attention.

"My life and decisions are my own. I'm telling you my plans because you're my family and I love you—but I won't tolerate interference in my future happiness. What happened was a mistake, a one-night thing. I refuse to make the situation worse by marrying Jake."

Though she'd spoken quietly, the silence in the living room couldn't be louder if she'd set off a firecracker. Every gaze swiveled to where she sat, pale but composed.

"Want to bet? You'll do the right thing," Glenn growled. His face was flushed, his eyes dark with intense emotion, and he was obviously itching for a fight.

Laila smiled at him, gently and sadly. "Hayley Jesmond," was all she said. Jake hadn't a clue what the local land owner Ben Jesmond's gorgeous and still single sister had to do with anything; but Glenn clearly did. He flushed, and his aggression visibly lowered.

"That was different," he muttered, looking at his feet.

"Why?" she said softly. "Because she lost the baby—or because it was you stuck in this situation? You're saying you have the right to choose your life partner, but I don't?"

Andrew growled, "Seems to me you did choose him, Lai. Everyone with eyes that night saw you choose him." Andrew watched Laila flush with no small amount of satisfaction—and Jake was feeling the same. Whatever she said, that was a truth she could never deny. She'd wanted him, and she'd got him, not the other way around. "So what's changed since then?"

For the first time, her gaze fell. She plucked at her loose jade-green dress—the first dress Jake had ever seen her wear—before she looked around her father to Marcie, her eyes pleading for understanding. "I want what you and Dar have." Her voice was barely above a mumble, but the passion in her bubbled through each word. "I don't want my husband to put up with me. I'd rather die than go through a shotgun wedding with a man who sees my baby and me as a mess he has to clean up!"

Barely realizing it, Jake flinched. Would she never stop punishing him for that word?

She's not punishing you, fool. Can't you see? a voice inside his head whispered. *She truly believes it.*

Yeah, he'd done a perfect job of turning Laila away from him; and how to bring her round again he didn't know. His vows to care and protect them both only seemed to put her off; his passion garnered a response every time, but it didn't sway her to his way of thinking.

So what did women want? What made them happy, apart from a vow of love and happy ever after he couldn't in all honesty give her?

"Well? Aren't you going to say something, Connors?" Brian

Robbins demanded roughly, interrupting his reverie. "Is what she says true?"

Jake looked Brian straight in the eye. "Anything I said or felt before the baby is irrelevant. I want to marry her, and give our child my name."

Brian's brow lifted. "I think the Robbins name is a good enough one for any grandchild of mine—and obviously to Laila whatever you said or did to hurt her *is* relevant. So you don't think her feelings are important?"

How was he supposed to answer that? Of course he cared about her feelings—far more than he was going to admit, with an emotional Laila ready to pounce on anything positive he said and make him her hero…and her lover.

He hadn't deserved that miracle first time around, and he deserved it even less now, no matter how much he ached for it, day and night. Aching for Laila was his personal penance for being fool enough to make love to her, and he'd take the punishment.

In the face of the impossible—*three* blunt-spoken and too-perceptive people who saw straight through his stoic stance to the truth—he kept his mouth shut.

Robbins asked gruffly, "What kind of husband would that make for her…or for any woman? How do you expect her to think she could marry you when she knows you don't care about her?"

"I didn't say that," he growled. "I will do my dead-level best to keep her and the baby safe and happy—"

Robbins cut through his little speech with a voice like a machete. "Bunkum. The lot of it's just so much talk. What do you feel for my girl?"

The entire Robbins clan looked at him with extreme interest in the answer.

Except for Laila. She sat still and stared at her lap. She was flushed with embarrassment—no, he knew it was worse than mere discomfort when he saw her swipe at a tear trickling down her cheek: she was *ashamed*. Preparing herself for the humiliation she knew his answer would give in front of the people she loved and esteemed most.

God help him, would he never stop hurting her, this beautiful woman who'd never done anything but give to him, without taking a thing back? If they were alone right now, he'd take her in his arms and show her how good second best could be for them both…

If he hadn't sworn to her he wouldn't do just that. But he'd broken that vow so many times—just about every time he saw her—she wouldn't think a thing about it anymore. He'd lost the ability to keep his hands off her from the moment she'd refused his proposal, and now he no longer knew if he did it to make her agree to marry him, or because he was branding her as his woman—or just because he couldn't help himself. Her silky skin, bright-as-the-sun smile and generous kisses lit up all the night-dark places inside him, and he was fast becoming addicted.

Becoming? He *was* addicted, had been from her first touch the night of the party, when the feel of her gentle fingers brought him out of the darkness of never-ending memory. But giving in to his hunger would open up a whole new world of pain and fear. He had to keep his distance.

"Well?"

Feeling like a germ under a microscope—and one not living up to anyone's expectations—he clung to the reiteration that felt like a broken record, even to him. "I'll marry her as soon as she agrees. I want to stand by her, to raise our child together."

"But she's right—you don't love her. Anyone can see it." Glenn stated it as a rough, blunt fact. "Why don't you love her? Everyone loves Lai! What more could you want? She's a great girl, and would be a fantastic wife. A hundred guys would kill to take your place!"

Something streaked through him like wildfire, and just as hot and blistering. Those guys had better stay away from Laila from now on. She was *his* woman, no matter what she said; and if those men even looked at his woman—

"Glenn, please," Laila whispered, sounding anguished, "please, stop it."

Startled, Jake looked at her. Seeing her face—like that day in the barn, so lost and broken—he couldn't hold out. He crossed the room, squatted in front of her and held her arms in his hands. "It's all right." He caressed her arms in reassurance. "They have the right. I don't mind."

If anything, the heartrending sadness grew. She lowered her gaze and shook her head. Her hair fell across her face, hiding her emotions…but her hands were trembling.

He wanted to hit something—preferably his thick skull. Having seen so much of Laila's sweet bravado lately, how could he not know? How could he not have seen how much stress this family conference would put her through?

And yet still, she'd stuck to her guns. With the weight of family expectation burdening her shoulders, she wouldn't take the easy way out he'd offered her. She'd chosen truth over the pretty lie. She still refused to take second best, even under family pressure to marry.

He couldn't help but admire her strength of character. So many women would have folded by now, given in under the weight of expectation and the thought of support in parenting, if nothing else. Laila wanted love—but she was stuck with him now. If only he could make her see he was giving her all he had left—his fidelity, his name and a father for their child.

Second best. Shotgun wedding. I'm just a mess for him to clean up…

There was only one way to snap her out of her sadness now—but he couldn't kiss her in front of her family.

With gentle fingers, he tipped up her chin. "Laila, don't you understand?" he whispered. "It's not your problem. You're beautiful, sweet, caring and loyal—all a normal man could want." He shook his head, wishing he knew what to say to her. "It's not you."

But her eyes wouldn't meet his. Sitting there so lost and alone, like one of those sad-faced china dolls with broken-hearted eyes that Sandy had loved as a girl.

He'd always hated those dolls…and still more, he hated the look on Laila. She was made for laughter and teasing, impudence and happiness, and he'd stolen it from her. He had to fix it.

Aching to reassure her, to bring back that joyous *life* that had drawn him to her from the start, he dropped a tender kiss on her cheek—it was wet—and one on her lips.

But after one sweet moment where she made that tiny, wonderful sound in her throat that told him she loved his touch, she pulled back. "I'm not a child to be placated with fairy tales or kisses better," she snapped. "Don't patronize me, Jake."

Well, the life had returned to her, all right. She could do with the joy that still wasn't there; but right now he'd take what he could get. She was no longer sad or passive—and that would do him for now…at least until they were alone.

He put his hands up in mock surrender. With a little smile he backed off, giving her space—and then remembered where they were.

Looking around with caution, he saw the knowing looks on every face in the room.

Brian Robbins wasn't grinning, but the nod of satisfaction spoke volumes, as if he'd seen something in the minute's byplay that he, Jake, hadn't. As if he thought…

What were they all thinking—? What had he given away? Had Laila seen? What did she think? He couldn't afford her to see any of the feelings growing in him. If she started to hope…

Now he was the one needing space; pins and needles flared

along every nerve ending. He got back to his feet and backed right away from her, keeping his gaze on Brian, because looking at Laila suddenly felt too dangerous.

But he discovered that Brian's gaze held as much to send gut-gnawing fear through him—for that look held knowledge.

Brian Robbins knew his real name.

Of course he knew—he'd probably always known. Brian Robbins would have every potential employee thoroughly checked out, for a criminal past if nothing else. He wouldn't allow any ex-cons near his wife and kids without knowing it— and Jake wouldn't have come one step inside the house while Laila was there if Brian hadn't known every part of his background.

Who he was. His marital status, home, family and financial records. Brian probably knew his entire history—*including Jenny and Annabel.*

Don't go there. Focus on the present, or you'll lose Laila and the baby.

And though the rational part of him knew that was probably the best solution for them, he couldn't be rational about Laila. He wished to God he could, but the sweetness of her, her life and light was filling up every dark corner of him, making him hope and want things he ought never hope to have.

It seemed Brian hadn't told Laila about Jenny and Annabel—yet. He had to tell her first; but the very thought of it made his gut churn. He just didn't know if he could do it. What would she think of him?

"Let us know when we can start arrangements for the wedding," was all Brian said—but the words were as much threat as promise. *Marry my girl.*

"Anytime's fine with me," he said quietly, willing Brian to feel the commitment he'd made to Laila; but he hadn't reckoned with Laila's reaction to his words.

She shot to her feet, her face white and strained. "Well, isn't that wonderful. You two work it all out, no doubt with Glenn and Drew's input. Don't forget to tell me where to show up, dress on and smile in place—because that's all I'm good for. It's obvious that my wishes don't count in this shotgun wedding— not with any of you. But don't throw engagement parties and bridal showers. If you expect me to smile and be happy in front of everyone, or to keep our dirty little secret, you're wrong, because I *will* tell the truth if you force me into this."

The silence was absolute because they all knew she meant every word.

"Lai, we only want what's best for you," Andrew said, his voice rough with caring.

She turned on her brother with a fierceness Jake would have given anything to see in her moments ago. "What's *best* for me, Drew? A cover-up lie of a wedding so that nobody talks about the mighty Robbins clan, or remaining a single mother, going through the gossip, and waiting to find the man who'll actually care about me? Is looking good in the community more impor- tant to you than whether I'm happy?" Her voice cracked on the last word.

Nobody dared answer that emotional bomb.

She almost stumbled as she left the room. Jake ran to help her, but she almost fell again avoiding him. "Not you. *Not you!*"

The door closed behind her with a small click that hit Jake like a gunshot.

He turned for the door, intending to follow her, to have it out.

At that moment Marcie stood up, her slim, tough Outback woman's form taut. "I'll go to her. None of you will listen in." She looked at each man in turn, and her unspoken reproach left them all wilted, feeling ashamed and inadequate. "And not one of you—not you—" glaring at her husband "—or you—" she nodded at Jake "—will nag her again. She needs time to think about what she wants, and no men telling her what will make her happy. Not one of you has a clue."

"Stop it, Marcie," Brian snapped. "It's Laila that doesn't know how it feels to be a single parent. I do—and I'd never wish those years of fear and loneliness on a child of mine."

"Yet you never thought twice about wishing it on Hayley Jesmond when she and Glenn broke up eight years ago. You advised him to not marry her because he was only twenty, and sent him away on business, leaving Hayley to lose the baby, thinking Glenn didn't love her," his wife interrupted him, her voice implacable. Flushing, Brian turned involuntarily to Glenn, whose white, averted face told of a pain that hadn't subsided after eight years—as much pain as Laila's face had shown a few minutes before. "Your children are adults, Brian. Let them make their decisions—right or wrong, the decisions belong to them."

Brian's face was a conflicting mixture of shame and mutiny. "But I don't want her hurt!"

"She's already hurting, and you don't have the power to change that," she replied, with a glance at Jake. "If you go to her, I daresay she'll let you have your piece with her. You might even get your way—but you can't guarantee her happiness, or force this young man to have feelings for Laila that may never come." She sighed. "Brian, she can't live under your shadow anymore. She came home to us in her time of need. Don't drive her away now, by forcing her into a life she's terrified will destroy her."

She walked out, opening the door and closing it as quietly as Laila had…leaving the men as dazed and bewildered as if they'd survived a sudden blitz. And it was, really: the overwhelming knowledge that they, the mighty men of the last frontier, were wrong.

Jake looked around at the Robbins men. Yeah, they had the same astonished look he knew was on his face. Outspoken or quiet, the Robbins women were a formidable duo. With Marcie on her side, Jake was betting he wouldn't be seeing Laila in a wedding dress anytime soon.

He set his jaw. No matter what it took, his child would bear his name—and his child's mother was going to be his wife.

No matter what it took to get Laila to marry him, he'd do it—even play dirty. He wasn't going to lose. Not this time.

CHAPTER FIVE

"WHAT do you think you're doing?"

Startled, Laila pulled on Starfire's reins, turning around to face Jake, who stood at the edge of the exercising paddock, his face taut and challenging. Her brows lifted. "What I do every day, exercising the horses. Wallaby is a working station, you know," she reminded him with gentle humor. "I've done it all my life."

There was no lightening of his grim face. These days his anger and anxiety seemed carved in dark marble. "Not anymore." He grabbed her hips and lifted her from the saddle with expert knowledge, dislodging her feet from the stirrups without a hiccup in his movement, sliding her down over his body and to the ground.

It was a superb movement; it might even have been romantic, but for her fast-rounding belly sliding against him instead of her once slender shape—and the seeming lack of awareness on his part that she'd touched his body at all.

"You're not riding anymore, apart from basics in the paddock close to the house."

Expecting the dictum, she didn't gasp—if she gave any sign of weakness now, he'd win. She stepped back and planted her hands on her hips. "I hope you have the doctor's signed statement forbidding riding for me? Otherwise you can take a hike. I don't obey you."

"You will obey me in this," he retorted, leading Starfire back to her stall, much to the horse's obvious displeasure. "I'll talk to Brian about it if I have to. Last I checked the horses were part of Wallaby, and not for your personal riding pleasure."

Laila stalked after him into the stable. "Last I checked you were a jackaroo, an employee, not the manager or the owner—and I don't ride for mere pleasure," she snapped, hurt at the implication that he still saw her as the Princess. "Starfire isn't a working horse—she's a breeding mare, and she's *mine*. I bought, bred and reared her at our Ghost Gum estate. She's thrown two champions so far, and interest in breeding with her is rising. She needs to keep in shape."

"Colin can ride her from now on." He unhitched the saddle and pulled it from the horse, hanging it on the wall.

"So can I," she said implacably, grabbing the saddle and preparing to resaddle Starfire.

His expression turned as dark as night thunder. "Don't do it, Laila."

About to snap back, she looked deeper—and saw the haunting fear beneath the anger in his face. So taut, holding it all inside some cavern in his soul…but feeling so much beneath the mask he chose to show to the world. "Give me a good reason, and I'll think about it."

"Riding puts the baby at risk. You're almost a vet—you should know that!"

Slowly she shook her head. "That's a fallacy, Jake," she said quietly. "All studies done in the past few years show that, while cross-country training and showjumping can have some risk, normal riding—cantering, not galloping—carries no risk to the mother or child."

Obviously about to argue, he stopped and stared hard at her. "You've looked it up?"

"Of course I have. I want this baby to be safe and well." Though she was tired and her tummy felt tight, wearing her out faster than she'd ever dreamed, she spoke with all the patience and reason she could muster. Something was going on here that she didn't understand, and she wanted to. "It was one of the first things I asked Dr. Broughton."

"He's a specialist, right?" Jake's voice was somehow portentous of something deeper.

She nodded. "He's an obstetric surgeon who works out of Bathurst and Dubbo."

"He knows your case."

"Yes, of course. He saw me for four months."

"And our local Flying Doctor?"

"I saw him last week." She shrugged, wishing she knew where he was heading with this; but she hadn't slept well last night, and her head felt stuffed with clouds. "You know how it is out here. They're fantastic, and they have copies of Dr. Broughton's notes, but you take the doctor who comes to the clinic, or the midwife, unless complications arise—but so far none have. It's been a textbook pregnancy."

"Textbook pregnancies can turn on a pin to become deadly. The death rate out here is ten times that of towns with facilities. You've been warned of that?"

"Of course I have, but I'm an Outback girl—and we Robbinses are tough. I know the risks." She frowned. "What's your point, Jake? It's obvious you have one."

"The same point I made a few weeks ago." He took her hands in his, his gaze searching hers. "I want us to move to Bathurst until the baby's a few months old, at least. Until you finish your course, if that's what you want. I'm well able to support us."

Her frown grew. She felt lost between the urge to snap, to warn him against trying to take her independence from her, and following the instinct screaming at her that there were deeper waters here, with rips and eddies she didn't understand. The fact that he was touching her at all showed that he felt very strongly about this. He wasn't trying to seduce her—he was in deadly earnest. "My grandfather left me enough to live on for the next twenty years. I haven't touched any since I first bought furniture for my flat in Bathurst. Money isn't the issue, Jake. I'd like to know what your real problem is."

A muscle tic began beside his mouth before he clamped his teeth together. His eyes burned, yet were as cold as a winter night. A minute passed until he spoke. "You and the baby will be safe. I won't let anyone—even you—put you or the baby in danger."

There was that vow again—and those deep, cold undercurrents were pulling her under. "What has that to do with this moving to Bathurst idea?"

He looked at her as if she'd lost her marbles. "You and the baby need to be near good facilities. A good maternity ward, with an obstetrician and surgeon close at hand. Out here you're hours from help."

She shook her head, trying to clear it. With every word he spoke he confused her more. "Dr. Broughton is only at Bathurst twice a month. It's only places like Sydney or Melbourne, or the bigger coastal cities like Newcastle, that have those facilities on tap."

"Then we'll move to Sydney."

Now she did gasp. "You're crazy. Nothing would induce me to move to a big city!"

"We can go to Newcastle, then." He nodded, with a look of satisfaction in his eyes. "That's only about an hour's drive from the Ghost Gum estate, right? That's only fifteen minutes by air. You'd be more settled there."

"More like two hours. Ghost Gum's on the northwestern fringes of the Hunter Valley."

He made a savage sound. "Stop putting up roadblocks, Laila. This is going to happen."

"Only if you make it happen by abduction, Connors, because I won't go willingly." She backed off when he reached out to touch her. "Don't. It won't work. I won't be shoved around like a pawn on your chessboard. Don't expect me to go anywhere with you while you're still locking me out of your life and your reasons for packing me up and taking me from my home."

"I wanted to take you to Bathurst—that was your home for seven years," he growled, taking a step toward her, then another and another, his eyes gleaming with the sensual intent that told her he was going to kiss her into it if he could.

And she hated the way she'd already gone breathless and flushed. Waiting, *waiting*.

"Laila." He growled still, but soft, predatory. And he was so beautiful.

Need slammed into her, scrambling her argument. What had they been talking about, and did it matter, anyway? Everything she wanted was right here in front of her...

She swayed into him, lost. Her eyes fluttered shut as he brought her into his arms.

The raw, scorching passion she'd hungered for still wasn't in evidence—but oh, the tender nibbling on her lips, along her jaw, and the fluttering kisses on her throat, were more than enough—somehow so exquisite, it was more than she could take. Her knees almost gave way. "Oh, Jake," she whispered, holding on tight to him, in case he disappeared on her again.

He whispered back as he held her up and close against him. "Come with me to Bathurst, Laila. You won't regret it."

If he'd shorn through her sensual haze with a pair of wool shearers he couldn't have ripped it apart more effectively; but being Laila, she wouldn't give in or back down. She stood on her tiptoes until her mouth was against his ear. "No, Jake," she whispered back.

His sigh was the last thing to touch her skin before he gently released her. "You're making this harder than it needs to be."

"No, *you* are." She held him off with an upraised hand.

"Don't manipulate me—just tell me why. Tell me your real reasons for taking me away from my family, and I promise you, I'll think about it."

Without a word he turned and stalked off toward the shearers' quarters; but the paleness of his skin, and his dark, burning eyes, told her far more than his lips ever had.

Without warning, a sudden, rippling pain gripped her lower belly. She gasped, grabbing hold of where her baby rested, panic slaking through her. "Jake…"

Her voice was too soft for him to hear—and she was going to fall down any moment. The quivering pains were growing stronger by the moment.

"Jake…"

He turned, and was running to her in moments. "Laila!" As she started to crumple he was there, lifting her in his arms; but his look of utter panic didn't reassure her. "What is it?"

"Pain," she whispered, her eyes fluttering shut. She couldn't help him now; she had to concentrate. Her hands held tight to her belly. *Stay in there, my little man. Stay safe with your mummy. Don't go, my baby!*

She felt him running—probably toward the house, to get help…but he didn't jerk her, not once. He carried her as if she were something precious.

He laid her down somewhere cool and comfortable moments later. "We're in the clinic room, Laila." A soft sound, and the blinds were closed. "I'm calling the Flying Doctors and your obstetrician—but I need to check for spotting or bleeding." He said the last word as if he'd forced it out of a closed throat. "I need to do it now. I need to know what's going on with you."

She knew she should be embarrassed, to say he had no right to check her so intimately—she should insist he call Marcie. But all she did was nod. She had to know, now. Her baby, her sweet, lovely baby…he had to be safe!

And like it or not, Jake *did* have the right. She'd given him the right by taking him to her bed, and conceiving this baby. This was his child, too, his life and future.

Her maternity jeans were peeled from her hips and down her thighs with exquisite care. Her panties followed, and she felt no embarrassment, only the all-consuming fear for her baby—a feeling she knew he shared. They were together on this. She wasn't alone.

He checked her underwear, and gave a gentle sigh. "No bleeding." With infinite tenderness, he replaced her clothing— but he lifted her maternity top to reveal her rounded stomach. "Hang in there, little one," he whispered. "We'll get the doctor for your mummy. We'll make this right." And slowly, gently, he kissed the mound of her pregnancy, then again.

He lifted his face and looked at Laila, his eyes filled with a tender longing she'd never seen in him—and he leaned down again to kiss her mouth. "We'll get through this, Laila. I swear everything will be all right."

Foolish tears rushed to her eyes. She opened her arms to him, and they held each other for a very long time.

Finally, reluctantly it seemed, he straightened. "I'm going to get your father and Marcie now." He covered her with the standard-issue cell blanket, and turned on the air-conditioning unit. "Don't move. Just rest, Laila. I'll be back soon."

If she had to pass one more boring day doing nothing, she'd head back to Bathurst on the first flight…if she weren't certain Jake would be on that same flight, or the one following.

They were all driving her crazy—especially Jake. So far he'd flown Dr. Broughton up here to examine her, hired a permanent midwife to stay at Wallaby until the baby's birth—or, as he'd said, until she agreed to go somewhere safer—and all but locked her in the house, citing the baby's safety every time she put a foot out of doors without a companion.

What would be next...security cameras to follow her every move?

Laila blew out a sigh of frustration. For the past ten days, since Dr. Broughton had pronounced her cramps to be a stronger than normal form of the common Braxton-Hicks contractions and put her on medication, it seemed everyone was in league against her. She couldn't ride, couldn't help with grooming or fencing, and roundups were absolutely out. Dr. Broughton hadn't said a word about constant rest; the family had taken his words that way. Marcie's four miscarriages had left her paranoid; Dar was clucking around Laila day and night. Jake checked on her every hour. If it was up to Jake she'd never leave the house—or her bed. Dar had put Jake on duties near the house, so her incarceration could be permanently enforced.

One incident of cramps the doctor said were perfectly normal in the second trimester, if hers were stronger than usual—and Jake was her personal bodyguard...no, her *bulldog*, growling if she moved out of doors. Glenn and Andrew were in on the conspiracy.

Laila didn't feel cherished; she felt smothered. It was enough to make her wonder if they all thought she was the first person on earth to ever get pregnant.

It could have been touching to think Jake felt such concern...if she could believe his concern was for her, instead of all for the baby. But since the time they'd held each other in the clinic, he'd withdrawn again. He fussed over her, gave her physical and emotional support, was always worried about something, but his heart wasn't there—at least not for her. She was the carrier of Jake Connors's baby, and the Robbins clan's first grandchild. Nothing more.

So here she was, stuck inside the house for the first time in her outdoor-loving life, allowed out for two half-hour walks every day. She was ready to throttle someone. Jake, for preference, though right now, Dar, Drew or Glenn would also do nicely.

At this moment she was reduced to mixing cakes for Marcie, ordering the catering and doing all the traditional female things for the nonengagement "baby celebration" party—Dar's over-the-top concession to her feelings. *You think we're ashamed to show your pregnancy in front of the community? We'll show you! We'll show them all.*

Such a Robbins thing to do. If you can't have it your way, pretend to the hilt that it *is* your way. Dar had called her bluff in spectacular style, before the whole community—and she was sure Jake was in on the plot somehow. *Let's see how long she holds out from the wedding, when the whole community knows...*

She refused to buckle. She'd go along with the party— she'd even make the best cake and the best aperitifs she could. Since she was about to become a mother, she needed to know how to cook, and Marcie was the best. But Dar was in for a few surprises tonight—and so was Jake.

Later that afternoon, Laila twisted the chains back and forth to make the swing twirl, watching the sun fall in the last hour before the guests began arriving.

Her bum was barely fitting into the swing anymore. She'd expected to grow, breasts and tummy, but why were her hips spreading already? And as for those little dimples coming up...! Soon she wouldn't fit on the swing at all, or in her bed. She'd have to buy a new one.

What does that matter? You sleep alone anyway, no matter what size bed you get.

"I've been looking for you."

She didn't bother to turn around; the voice, dark and hot as a night fire, was permanently imprinted on her senses, her own personal torture: she was always unable to reach out to really touch that beautiful fire.

"You and everyone else." She twirled the swing again, enjoying the comforting familiarity of twisting from side to side. A collective screech came overhead, as cockatoos flew from tree to tree, finding their night nests.

"Feeling crowded, are you?"

She shrugged. "It won't hurt the baby if I indulge in some emotion."

The old swing creaked as he twisted the chain so the swing—and Laila—turned to face him. "Have you thought about what I said? About relocating to Bathurst until the baby's born?"

The bulldog was back, trying to take her last bone from her. Heaven knew she didn't want to be here, smothered to screaming point—but—

She frowned, keeping her gaze on the sunset sky. So lovely, rich and colorful—and *free*. Through a tight throat, she whispered, "I think I'd be lonely there. I'd hate to be there with all my classmates finishing in a few months, too busy to see me, and without the family."

"You'd have me," he reminded her quietly.

She nodded. "Like I said, I'd be lonely."

Having thrown her emotional bomb, she waited for the inevitable coldness and withdrawal from her; instead, she got a thoughtful, "I know it must hurt not finishing this year, Laila—but you *will* finish your course. I'll make certain of it."

Her throat thickened, thinking of going back there without Jodie, Danni and Jimmy. Living as the Princess all over again, with no friends, no love…

A gentle touch to her cheek snapped her out of her reverie. "You look as though you've lost your last friend," he said, with genuine caring in his voice. "Want to talk about it?"

Laila looked up, filled with sudden, blazing hope, but it died within seconds. He was doing everything so right, yet it all felt wrong. He was leaning over her, his gaze on her, his entire attention on what she wanted—but while his eyes held concern, it was cool; his hands were back on the chain, inches from her own hands.

He might care, but his caring was light-years from the love and tenderness she needed, and hadn't once seen since the day she'd had the pains. Giving everything to her except the one thing that would ensure her well-being: his heart.

His self-protection was like a shield made of steel, it was so cold, so hard and implacable.

"Time to get ready for the party. Were you sent out to make sure I don't embarrass everyone by turning up in something inappropriate?" She sighed and plucked at the big, loose shorts. "No need to worry. I can't fit into anything but maternity stuff anymore, and it's all the pretty stuff Marcie bought for her last baby."

"You know that's not why I came out here."

Gripping the chain tighter, she kept her voice level. "I haven't done anything strenuous. I've taken my vitamins, eaten my fruit and vegetables, had my two liters of water, and had a walk. I didn't go near the horses. I didn't leave the grounds. The baby is fine."

"Laila."

She turned her head away at the quiet rebuke in his voice. Oh, no, that stupid weepy thing was about to happen, and she'd rather die than cry in front of him again. "What have I done wrong this time? I'm doing everything the doctor said to do. I'm sitting around, bored to tears day and night. What else do you want from me?"

The quiet stretched out over time, maybe moments only, but she felt ready to scream by the time he finally spoke. "You're unhappy, Laila."

Wrapping her arms around the chains, she pulled them together to interlace her fingers. "Oh, gee, and I thought I was doing such a good job of hiding it."

"Let me help you, Laila. Tell me what's wrong. Is it your course? You want to go back and take pickup classes until the baby's born? We can do that. We can do anything you want."

She shook her head, trying so hard not to cry. Living here

with him nearby was bad enough, but living with him, knowing he didn't love her…

She cried out as he released the swing and she shot around, overcompensating the rotation once, twice. Then he grabbed it again from the other side, lower down as he squatted before her. "Come on, Laila, please. What do you need?"

You want the list? Unbearably tempted to let it all out now that somebody was listening, she opened her mouth—then she made a fatal error.

She looked in his eyes…the eyes that had been holding her captive from the first day; and only saw guilt. The totally self-contained, responsible man thinking *I did this to her and I have to fix it*. He wasn't even trying to manipulate her now; he really did care. But he didn't even know that his guilt was standing between him and everything he wanted from her, like the ancient cherubs with flaming swords forever barring the way to Eden.

What was the point?

"Nothing," she said dully. She jerked at the chains until he released them; then she got to her feet and walked on unsteady feet past him and into the house. "It's time to get ready."

Her pretty, rounded form was bathed in the falling sun, her hair on fire, her skin warmed by its touch—and yet it was a lie, for while she was beautiful, she was cold, so cold.

Jake watched her go, a strange, hot ache filling him. He hated seeing her so unhappy all the time. Making her smile had lately become his obsession; but he didn't know what else to do to help her. Laila was locking him out—and it wasn't payback. She wasn't built that way.

It was merely that she'd learned about putting up barriers from the best teacher in the entire Outback—and he didn't have a clue how to lower them for her, when in five years he'd never found a way to lower his own.

CHAPTER SIX

THE curious had turned out in force tonight.

She'd counted about two hundred in the crush inside the house and spilling out over the verandas and backyard. The kegs of beer out the back were emptying rapidly, and the usual suspects were going for it in the sculling contest. The yard-glass was being passed from one guy to the next, getting a real workout. Half the local boys were unsteady on their feet already.

Meanwhile the women were getting their fill—of gossip and speculation. The local girls were unable to hide their glee.

The Princess had fallen off her pedestal…and with a common jackaroo, of all people!

Let's see the boys race after her now!

Laila pasted on a smile for the fiftieth time in the past hour as another couple came up for conversation, an introduction to Jake, who'd been hovering behind her every time someone asked to meet him—and to find out what news they could.

"The baby's due in late January or early February, Aunt Ellen," she said a minute later to her mother's old friend's brilliant opening gambit, one she'd heard dozens of times tonight: *You're pregnant!*

She answered the questions on the ultrasound results, but refused to say if the child was boy or girl. That knowledge belonged only to the immediate family for now. There was no certain confirmation of the baby's sex, anyway, except within her own heart.

"And this is the baby's father?" Ellen smiled, stretching her neck so she could get a clear view of the infamous jackaroo who'd destroyed the Princess's reputation.

"Yes, this is Jake Connors." Laila stepped aside for Jake to come forward. He shook hands with Ellen and her husband, Tom, smiling a little and saying all the right things.

Until Ellen asked the one question he couldn't answer: the same question everyone over the age of forty had been asking all night.

"So when is the wedding?"

No matter how much she'd prepared for it, the smile still froze on her face. "Have you heard any news about a wedding, Aunt Ellen?"

"If I had, I wouldn't need to ask," the square-built lady with a kind face chided gently.

It took all her willpower not to gulp at the kind of rebuke her mother might have made, or Marcie. "Then you know as much as we do. We're in the twenty-first century, Aunt Ellen. Have a lovely night. The cheesecake is really good."

She made her way through the crowd, nodding and smiling, continuing to answer the same questions in the same way, a silent, stoic Jake by her side. And if tears stung her eyes, it was only at the back of them; she didn't let the emotion gather. If it hurt to have her second-deepest wish repeated every five minutes, she wasn't going to show it.

Even the utter joy that was an Outback wedding wasn't worth it. Not without love.

Never without love.

"So much for your grand plan," Marcie said softly to Brian.

He growled something indistinct as he watched the night

unfold, and to none of his expectations. Laila was dressed in a pretty maternity dress, hair pulled back in a braid, and seemed happy to share her baby news with any interested friend or avid gossip he'd invited tonight. She introduced Jake to everyone as the father—but so far she'd refused to give in to any hinted or even open speculation regarding their wedding plans; and it seemed that Jake was taking care of all her needs without throwing the spanner into the works Brian had expected. "She's as stubborn as her mother was."

Marcie smiled and squeezed her husband's hand. "Her mother? Oh…"

Distracted, Brian grinned at his wife. "Are you calling me stubborn, woman?"

"If the hat fits," she replied, laughing.

Laila heard floating snatches of their conversation as she walked by, but felt little urge to smile. Dar enjoyed a battle with a worthy opponent—but he wasn't used to losing against his daughter. Dar wasn't exactly a chauvinist, but Outback life was tough and the men tougher. Women out here fought their battles and won, just as the men did—but they stuck together against the odds. *Families* stuck together. The extremes of weather, the recurring droughts and crop failures, hospital, school, town and bank closures made all Outback people band together against common enemies. In that harsh yet old-fashioned world, a son—or, in particular, a daughter—didn't stand against a father's will.

Well, people said new experiences were nourishment for the soul. Dar should be feeling very filled by now.

A low growl drifted into her ear as soon as they were out of earshot. "Proud of yourself?"

She should have known Jake wouldn't let it pass. She kept walking toward the front of the house, her current refuge now that the stables were out of bounds, knowing he'd follow her out. "There's nothing to be proud about. We Robbinses don't take well to manipulation—or outright coercion. Dar should have expected this." She turned her head to look at him, lifting a brow. "Maybe you found it surprising, though."

He gave her the lopsided grin that twisted her belly in knots. "I'm not a steer to be roped in by your dad, Laila."

"I'm well aware of that," she retorted in her driest tone. "I almost felt sorry for him when he was trying to get you to invite your family here for tonight."

At that he chuckled, and touched her chin. "I never thanked you for that."

She didn't ask for what. She knew he'd been surprised by her discretion, in keeping her knowledge that he did have a family to invite. "No need. I believe in a person's right to privacy—and personal choice," she added softly as she opened the old, painted door to the veranda.

She sat down on the padded, canopied double swing, looking out into the night.

The swing creaked as he sat beside her…close, too close, yet the distance seemed stronger. "Was that shot aimed at me?"

If he didn't know, she wasn't about to enlighten him; she was tired of doing all the emotional work for him. "It's so dark and still tonight. The air is sad…full of ghosts."

"Don't say that!"

The sharp tone unnerved her. "Oh, good, another order to add to my growing list of don'ts and do's. I was wondering when it would come. It's been at least four hours since my last one." She got to her feet. "It's not as nice out here as I'd hoped. Can you tell them I'm tired? Since everyone wants me to rest, I'll take advantage of it."

He jerked to his feet, and put a hand on her arm. "Laila, I'm sorry. I didn't mean to—"

She turned to look up at him. "I give you your privacy. I've done everything you've told me to do—" apart from marrying you, or going anywhere to live with you on our own, and

Get FREE BOOKS and FREE GIFTS when you play the...

LAS VEGAS
GAME

Just scratch off the gold box with a coin. Then check below to see the gifts you get!

YES!
I have scratched off the gold box. Please send me my **2 FREE BOOKS** and **2 FREE GIFTS** for which I qualify. I understand that I am under no obligation to purchase any books as explained on the back of this card.

316 HDL EF45   116 HDL EF55

FIRST NAME

LAST NAME

ADDRESS

APT.#

CITY

(H-R-02/07)

STATE/PROV.

ZIP/POSTAL CODE

| 7 | 7 | 7 | Worth TWO FREE BOOKS plus TWO BONUS Mystery Gifts! |

www.eHarlequin.com

Worth TWO FREE BOOKS!

TRY AGAIN!

Offer limited to one per household and not valid to current Harlequin Romance® subscribers. All orders subject to approval.

▼ DETACH AND MAIL CARD TODAY! ▼

breaking my heart "—so please do the same for me," she uttered with more emotion than she'd felt in days. "I realize I'm the carrier of your child, all right? I know you want the baby safe. But for once can you please think about *me*, and what I want or need?"

He moved closer to her. His head bent to hers. Low, intense, he muttered, "Tell me."

If she gave in to his kiss now, she'd only lose again: lose another part of herself to this man who had everything she could ever want, but withheld the one thing she needed. "What's the point?" she asked wearily. "I speak, and instead of listening, you look at my belly. That's all that matters to you."

His face stilled. Something raw washed over his features for a moment. He held her shoulders, slowly caressing her, and she shivered.

His gaze darkened. Then he muttered, low and intense, "It's not all that matters. Tell me what you want, Laila, what you need. I swear I'll find a way for you to have it."

"I want," she stated clearly, stepping out from under his hands, "for everyone to leave me be. Give me a few hours to be Laila, not just the vessel carrying this child."

His hand dropped.

Laila pushed through the crowd, but saw none of them. She had to escape—she needed—

"Hey, Your Worship, I'm getting tired of your not noticing my presence, after I risked life and limb all the way from Bathurst in the poor ol' Valiant, to surprise you."

Laila stopped in her tracks, blinking to make the mists clear from her eyes. *Your Worship*? Only one person called her that, a gentle joke against the other students' sarcastic Princess Laila tag. Surely it couldn't be—

She looked up. Blocking her path was a young man with a dark, handsome face, messy dark curls, a grin as wide as the

Simpson Desert, and liquid black eyes with sooty lashes…
"Jimmy!" she squealed, and jumped into the big man's open
arms. "You came." And then she burst into tears.

"Hey, hey." Her best friend from university, and coworker
at the steakhouse, patted her on the back, holding her gently.
"What up, Your Worship? What they been doing to you? Want
me to hit anyone?"

"Get me out of here," she whispered. "Please…"

Jake stood frozen not five feet behind, watching the young
man he'd absently noticed but taken to be a new jackaroo
somewhere, shepherd Laila out of the house.

Laila didn't notice that she passed within inches of him. All
the awareness—the amazing feeling of knowing that Laila
always knew when he was near her, and her rich femininity
came surging into her eyes, her face, and her touch—wasn't
in evidence. All her concentration was for the man she'd hailed
with such joy. Her arm was wrapped around him as if she was
terrified he'd vanish if she let go for a moment.

Who was the guy? What was he to Laila? Why didn't he
know anything about him? And why did he touch Laila as if
he had the right to come within a mile of the woman who was
carrying his child?

When the two had left the house, Jake flicked a glance at
her family. They knew who the guy was, by the grim looks on
their faces. Brian looked fit to burst a vein in his forehead.

And everyone invited to the party watched the tableau in a
deep interest that told him the bush telegraph would be buzzing
before the night was over.

"I have to get out of here, Jimmy. They're driving me crazy…"

They sat at the edge of the dam; the light from the full
moon, reflected on the water, lit them up with soft, ghostly
radiance. Standing behind a tree about twelve feet away, about
to crash their party of two, Jake felt himself freeze again.

The desperation in her voice arrested him. Everything Laila said lately had been so controlled, so restrained—giving nothing away. He'd become more and more frustrated at the walls she'd put up to protect herself from hurt—and felt unwilling empathy, knowing how she must have felt during all these months she'd been trying to break through to him.

Curiosity overcame scruples. He needed to know—he *had* to know what he'd done to make her turn from him.

"What's wrong, babe?"

"Everything." Laila's voice held a sob. "Everything's wrong, Jimmy."

"Go on." The man she'd called Jimmy had his arm around her shoulders; her head was resting against his chest, safe, warm—trusting. "I'm here. Get it all off your chest."

How many times in the past two weeks had Jake all but begged her to trust him, to talk to him about what was upsetting her, and received nothing in return?

But there was no hesitation now; she spoke to the guy with complete trust. "They all know me, Jimmy—I'm an outdoor girl. I always have been. But they've confined me to the house—no horses, no animals at all. I can't even take old Blue for a good walk—I get no exercise apart from two slow, careful walks every day. I have nothing to do but cook, sleep and watch TV. I can't even read—all I want to read is my uni readers, and that hurts."

"Well, surely they understand that?" Jimmy asked gently. "All you ever wanted was to become a vet, and you can't finish your final year. The reminders make you feel bad."

"Jake's offered for me to go back next year—but then I wouldn't have you, or Danni and Jodie…" Her words were thick with tears. "No friends, no one to talk to…"

"Surely he talks to you?" Jimmy said after a few moments.

"No," Laila gulped. "He talks *at* me. Barks orders at me. Yells at me."

Jimmy said, rich with laughter, "And he doesn't know yet that when anyone tells you to go right, you go left just to prove you can, after your dad ordering you around all your life?"

Laila chuckled, and buried her face in the guy's chest.

Jake closed his eyes and sighed. Hadn't she noticed his softened attitude the past week or more? Couldn't she see his "barked orders" were only to give the baby a good start in life?

"What about the family? They're with you, right? They know you've always wanted to be a vet."

She sighed. "They're too excited about the baby to think of me. To them it's like, well, I got pregnant and I want the baby, right, so the sacrifice is normal. This is what women do—we cook and clean, wash and have babies. And after one incident of cramps, I'm locked in the house! I feel like Rapunzel!" The tears were flowing now, judging by her hiccups. "I can't stand being cooped up doing nothing all the time—it's driving me nuts. And he's always *there*."

"Your boyfriend?" Jimmy asked quietly enough…but Jake heard the timbre of his voice change. Whatever Laila believed, this man's feelings for her ran deep. Very deep.

"He's not my anything, Jimmy," she said, so soft he had to strain to hear her. "I always knew he didn't love me, but I feel like I'm just a body bearing a child. Even when he kisses me, he's so cold—because he doesn't feel anything. He only talks nicely to me, or kisses me, as a means to the end he wants—and I have the only thing he wants. His child, bearing his name."

Jimmy's expletive was short, to the point—and one hundred percent accurate.

Oh God, help me. Help me… Jake hung on to the tree he stood behind. A savage pain ripped through him, as if she'd taken his heart and dissected it.

Stupid, stupid! He'd known of her obvious intelligence and deep sensitivity long before the night she'd come to him, but that night, seeing his pain and braving rejection to help him, he'd thanked God for her. For Laila.

Yet from the moment she'd told him about the pregnancy, terrified of history repeating and of losing another woman and baby, he'd done his dead level best to distance himself from all he felt for her. He'd blinded himself to the woman, looking for the Princess in her every act. Yet from the time she'd come to him in his time of desperate need, to not forcing the knowledge of her pregnancy on him, and her discretion in keeping the knowledge of his family quiet, everything she did, everything she was put the truth in letters of fire. Laila was an exceptional woman—and the greater danger he was in of falling in too deep, the greater a distance he'd put between them. Even when she'd needed him most, he'd given her attention and worry, but not caring, always so determined to protect himself from the possibility of—

Loss. Grief.

Love.

The kind of love that led to the rip-your-soul-from-its-body grief he'd give his life to never have felt…the kind of love he knew he could feel for Laila, if he let himself.

He refused to feel any part of it. He'd made his life plans after he'd lost Jen and Annabel, and he was sticking to them with the tenacity of a man terrified of—

"What are you still doing here?" Jimmy's words reflected the sudden wonder in Jake's mind. Why was a woman like Laila still here? Why hadn't she walked?

Another soft hiccup. "Until recently, I thought that beneath his coldness he needed me—that he'd looked past the reputation to see me. But he won't—and I'm becoming someone I don't recognize, Jimmy, always on guard, unhappy day and night. I can't live like this…"

Every single part of Jake was hurting. Laila, beautiful, strong, wise Laila had seen through him, just as she always had…but not knowing why he chose to withdraw, why he kept hurting her day after day, she'd begun to do the same to him.

Why wouldn't she? You've taken away everything that means anything to her. Her studies, her career prospects—even her one remaining joy: the outdoor life, and her beloved horses. You took everything from her to calm your own fears, and never once told her why.

It's for the baby's life, Laila—and for yours. I can't stand the thought of losing you both, now that I've finally got a chance to—

But every time he took one step forward, he leaped back two—and now Laila saw him as her enemy. In this moment of ruthless honesty, he couldn't blame her for that.

"Come here." Jimmy held out his other arm to her. "Seems to me you're in desperate need of a cuddle, Your Worship— and some fun, and in that order. Let's go for a night swim in the dam, eat something wild and irresponsible like the chocolate stash I have in the Valiant, and after this thing they call a party, we'll do some more talking. As much talking as you need, Laila. I'll sit and listen all night if you need to…and let's just see any of 'em try to stop us."

Silence for a moment; then she said, soft and sad, "Not yet, Jimmy. I can't go for a swim during the party. There's too much gossip as it is. I can't embarrass them. If I swim with you during my party, they'll start taking bets that you're the real father…"

"I wish," Jimmy said, with quiet, comical fervor—and Laila laughed, beautiful and strong and happy, as she hadn't done since the day she'd told him about the baby.

"You're a goof," she said, with real affection in her voice.

"Yeah, I know," Jimmy replied firmly. "But we're going swimming, sooner or later. I wanna see the sexiest pregnant woman ever, drenched in dam water and her makeup off. I didn't come four hundred miles for nothing."

Laila gave a watery giggle. "I'm so glad you came." She

turned in his arm and held him as tightly as her burgeoning body would allow. "I don't know what I'd do without you here."

"Of course I came," Jimmy said softly. "I'll always be here for you. No matter what. Even when you get pregnant to some dumb goof who's so blind he can't see the treasure he's got right in front of him."

"You have no idea how much I needed to hear that," she whispered back. Jimmy laid his chin on her hair...and the *dumb goof* listening in on the conversation stood rooted in shock, feeling all the force of irony.

He'd spent months pushing Laila away; and now, at *their* baby celebration party, she was reaching out to another man— a man with obvious and very deep feelings for her.

His child, *his son*, could end up calling that man Daddy— and again, he couldn't blame Laila. She'd been honest about her needs from the start, and he'd given her what he thought she wanted, but not a single thing she needed.

But the root cause of his shock, he realized—only *now*, when it seemed to be too late—that the fear of losing his rights to the baby wasn't the only massive change going on inside his heart. Laila, this baby, were on his mind day and night.

Jenny and Annabel were fading from their constant place in his mind.

Panic, utter and complete terror, filled him. He couldn't forget—he'd sworn to Jen that he'd always love her, always remember. He'd given his solemn vow to bring up their daughter with love and her memory.

He hadn't even been able to do that for her, or for Annabel. He'd failed his family in every possible way. The least he could do was to remember them—and keep the love alive; yet at this moment, all he could see in his mind was Jen's dying form, not her sweetness and life and laughter, or their moments of love...

If Jen was fading, it was Laila's fault, with her brightness and impudence, her outspoken wisdom and her vivid passion for living. She'd brought him back to life, dominated his thoughts and made him want to reach out again, even if it was only for the sake of the baby—

Liar. You want her so bad you forget the baby whenever she touches you.

He'd never thought this could happen to him, but it had. He'd loved Jenny with a warm, sensual, comfortable love that could have lasted a lifetime—but this violent *craving* he had for Laila ate at him until he was with her again. Touching her again.

He wasn't in love—there was no possible way he could be—but he seemed to need—

No! He didn't *need* Laila, or the hectic jumble of emotions she inspired in him—reminding him that while he was safe in this life, it wasn't *life*: he existed, but didn't live. He didn't *feel*, which was exactly what he'd wanted.

Laila had taken that from him, that safe, comfortable cocoon, and he resented it, resented her. He utterly refused to show her just how far he'd come from the man she'd met first, or the aching in him to be a man again—

Then why can't you stay away from her for longer than an hour?

The baby. He wanted his child, and Laila was carrying him.

Yeah, right. That explains why you can't keep your hands off her, the little voice inside him jeered.

He couldn't escape that single truth. It seemed that, for now, they were both locked in sensual thrall, with a mutual fascination and need for each other—but Laila had the courage and strength to admit it…and to not use him to gain her own ends. If she had any ends. All the Princess seemed to want was simple love and happiness.

Laila was a woman with strong feelings. Sooner or later, her heart-deep need to be loved would overrule any sensuality or security he could give her. She needed not just a lover, but a friend: someone to share her life with. And faced with this young, good-looking guy who teased and cuddled her and was obviously deeply in love with her, Jake couldn't fool himself. She had a man who wanted to give her all the things he couldn't.

She probably had dozens of friends, and a hundred guys who'd line up to take his place, just as Glenn had said; but his greatest threat was right here, right now.

She'd marry Jimmy if he kept pushing her away, if he didn't let her into his life—but God help him for the world's biggest jerk, he no longer knew how to stop locking the world out.

"Hurts, doesn't it?"

Jake turned to where the whisper came behind him. Andrew Robbins stood there, neither in satisfaction nor triumph, but a curious understanding. "Marcie wants to talk to you. Come on."

Jake whispered in fury, "I'm not leaving her with him!"

"If you blunder in now, you'll lose her." Andrew placed a hand on Jake's resisting shoulder. "I know her. She needs time, man—something none of us have given her since she told us about the baby. Jimmy's one of the good ones. He'll take care of her. She'll come back."

"What if she doesn't?"

"Then she was never going to," Andrew said, very softly. "She's not a sheep—you can't bark at her and expect her to go the way you want. We all know that's your baby in there, and she hasn't forgotten that, but if you push her any more she'll go with him—and he loves her, man. If Jimmy takes her out of here, she might give you full visiting rights, but she'll never come back. This is your last chance to get this right. Lai knows what *you* want. It's what *she* wants that she has to figure out. *She needs time.*"

He tugged at Jake's shoulder, and, without knowing why, Jake let Laila's brother lead him away. He needed time to figure out what to do next.

Failure wasn't an option. Not when his part in his child's life hung in the balance.

CHAPTER SEVEN

LAILA'S mobile phone began bleeping within forty-five minutes.

Lying on her back on Jimmy's jacket, melting a chocolate ball in her mouth and enjoying the rare luxury of silence, she chose not to hear the sound...until Jimmy touched her shoulder. "Looks like the cavalry's about to ride in," he whispered, pointing at the indistinct human form coming through the shadowed trees separating the dam from the house.

She giggled, then sighed. "Drat."

Jimmy shrugged and grinned. "I got a few days. I don't have to go anywhere until next weekend...that is, if your dear papa will allow me to hang around."

"Oh, he will," she replied grimly. "If he wants me to stay here, he will."

"Laila."

She swiveled around, feeling like a puppet pulled by wires she couldn't find. Jake spoke, and she obeyed. "Yes, Jake?" she answered levelly. "What can I do for you?"

He didn't come any closer. "Your dad's getting pretty hot under the collar," he said, his voice quiet, restrained. "It's your party and people are wondering why you're not there."

Ten possible retorts rose to her mind, but something in his tone stopped her—his words—and the fact that he hadn't moved closer, filling her with his physical presence.

He wasn't telling her what to do.

"I'll be in soon." She glanced at Jimmy, who was already on his feet, a look of exaggerated resignation on his face that was almost saintly—and she laughed again.

"I'll be in the house if you want anything."

"Thanks." Laila's frown deepened as Jake turned and walked back without a glance.

"That's the hovering non-boyfriend?" Jimmy whispered. "Maybe my coming did some good. Looks like he got the message."

Laila shrugged. She never knew what to make of the enigma that was Jake Connors. "Time to get back in there."

Jimmy grinned. "And won't the party girl be making a big entrance. How many, you reckon, will start thinking I'm the daddy?"

She elbowed him in the stomach with a return grin. "At least twenty—and every one of them will believe it. There isn't much else to interest people out here. Gossip's the number one choice for fun." She stood up, and grimaced as her sandals landed in a still-fresh horse pat. "Oh, great," she groaned, and leaned on Jimmy's shoulder as she pulled off the sandals.

Jimmy laughed. "Now she's a real walking cliché—barefoot and pregnant."

She mock-punched his arm, and held his hand as they walked through the trees and back to the house.

"So which of this lot is the guy's family?" Jimmy asked on the way up the veranda. He totally ignored the raised brows of several guests wandering around the front garden and path as they walked past. "Who in this crowd belongs to him?"

"None. These are all our people, apart from a couple of the guys over there." She let go of his hand and pointed to a group of jackaroos on the side veranda, uncomfortable in their best clothes, hanging around the open-air bar. "They're his friends from his last job."

She moved to open the screen door, but Jimmy grabbed her wrist. "No *family*? Is he an orphan or something?"

Laila shook her head, slowly, feeling disturbed as she hadn't before. "No. He has a brother and sister that I know of, and a mother."

"And they're not here? When it's a party to celebrate his baby?" Jimmy shook his head, looking stunned.

She felt his incredulity. It seemed she was seeing a lot of things she hadn't before, through Jimmy's eyes.

Jimmy had a massive family, and their gatherings tended to be shouting-only affairs. She'd gone to two with him, and came out swishing from the beers and tea given to her, ten pounds heavier from all the good food, and feeling crushed from all the hugs. Of course Jimmy wouldn't understand what motivated Jake to keep his family from...

From what?

She dropped her smelly sandals, pulled the screen door open, and marched in.

Half the room fell silent at her entrance. Beers stopped halfway to mouths; lips paused in gossip. Eyes grew large at her entrance: barefoot, hair loose, and a tall, dark stranger behind her.

Laila lifted her chin, daring anyone to ask. She just hoped nobody could see the pulse pounding in her throat as she walked past people without offering an explanation.

Ignoring all the speculative looks, and Dar's compelling stare, willing her to come over and explain herself, she sought out just one person.

She found him, not in his usual corner, but talking to a group of men by the bar; but like everyone else, he watched her now. Yeah, she'd really made an entrance this time. She might as well have taken that swim—the sensation couldn't be bigger.

She lifted a brow, her gaze remaining on him. After a long

moment the hooded look grew, but he nodded, put down the beer in his hand and headed toward her.

"Go for it, tiger," Jimmy's quiet whisper sounded in her ear, as she waited for Jake. "Give him hell."

Her fingers fluttered back to his, touching in gratitude. It was so good to have a friend like Jimmy at her back.

She walked out the door ahead of Jake, with a strange sense of destiny walking behind, treading softly in her bare footprints.

To Jake it wasn't destiny following her, it was doom. It had been coming on with a slow relentlessness he'd chosen to turn from—but now he could feel the hardening of Laila's heart, and sensed that whatever she was about to say would decide his future.

She waited to make it to her place of refuge, her childhood swing, and sat on it—her thighs instead of her butt—and swung a few times before she spoke. The glow touched her half-averted face, pale, translucent and lovely. Moonlight reflected soft reddish lights from her hair; her dress clung to her, showing her fuller breasts and ripening belly. He ached with something more than desire: a yearning he dared not name. Still he envisioned her cold, beautiful face turning to his with all the emotion she'd once been unable to hide, lifting for his kiss—

It wasn't going to happen. She had something to say, and being a prudent man, he knew when to shut up and wait. But her words seemed to fly out of nowhere—and they were nothing that he'd expected.

"Why aren't your family here? Why didn't you want to invite them tonight?"

Though her question had been restrained, the shock came to him from darker emotion lurking beneath. He noted that even as he jerked back, wanting to check to see if he was awake or dreaming. Laila had been so good at minding her own business until now—at least since her initial attempts to get to know him—this was the last question he'd thought she'd ask.

"I thought you said you believed in giving people their space," he said quietly, to give himself time to think. What on earth was he supposed to say? *I don't deserve my family because I killed my wife and child? I can't face their forgiveness until I can find a way to forgive myself?*

The swing came to a slow stillness. She didn't speak until it stopped altogether. "It's my business if I'm the reason for you not wanting your family to meet the mother of your child."

She wasn't looking at him, but forward into the night, her normal vivid passion for living gone. She was so pale in the autumn moonlight, so cold. It was as if she didn't want to know, but felt driven to ask against her will.

Jake stood still behind her. When she became like this—quiet, strong and insightful—facing her was almost painful, like looking into a mirror and seeing the ugliness of his past written on his face. Yet this time her insight wasn't turned on him, and realizing that made him see the truth with a clarity that hurt in a way he couldn't explain.

"You think I'm ashamed of you?" he asked, feeling as if she'd shoved her knuckles into his solar plexus. "Is that what you think of me?"

The one-shouldered shrug was almost defiant; she didn't even turn her head. The distance between them seemed to grow longer with every word she said. "I don't know what I think. I don't know you."

"I'm doing the best I can, Laila," he muttered, wishing they didn't have to keep coming back to that.

At that, she finally turned her head. Her eyes were dark, hollow—mirroring the turbulence in her soul. A reflection of all the emotion she was getting so good at hiding from him. "Are you? Or are you giving yourself permission to keep your distance?"

Slowly his fists clenched together in impotent defiance. He didn't have an answer, but he didn't need to: she knew.

At his silence she shrugged again. "You expect me to take you on trust, to hand you my future without a word spoken. All I know is that you took what I stupidly offered one night, you have a family you won't share with me and you want to do the right thing by your child."

"It's all I have," he said, blunt but hoarse. Was it truth, or was he lying to them both? Lost in a mass of emotions he didn't want to acknowledge, he had nothing else to say.

"If that's all you have, agreeing to anything you want from me would be committing emotional suicide."

She said it in the same tone she'd use for remarking on the weather; her face reflected the same lack of emotional input. Why did that frighten him so badly? Why did he feel as if he'd committed the unforgivable sin in being honest? "I can't change it, Laila. I wish I could."

"Who is she?" she asked quietly. Her eyes watched him in a tired kind of sadness, as if she already knew the answer. "Who's the woman you can't put behind you?"

Shutdown.

The pain shot through his chest. His throat closed up; he couldn't speak. The wounds never stopped bleeding, day and night. Even now, when Jen's face had begun to fade from the front of his mind, and he could barely remember the good times, he lay in agony on his bed at night, trying to remember everything he'd forgotten. Going through a day without thinking of Jenny and Annabel was a betrayal he couldn't stand. His wife and daughter were dead and there was nothing he could do to change that.

Nothing Laila could do would end the anguish, or change the facts. No matter how much he thought about her, or how much he wanted their child, the facts remained. She made him yearn and ache for a happiness he didn't deserve—unless time suddenly went backward and he could relive the decision to put his work before his family.

This is your last chance to get this right.

He spoke with a voice scratchy with his will fighting Laila's need. "This is my problem. You will meet my family one day. I'm not ashamed of you, Laila."

"Uh-huh." With a long creak, she'd hauled herself off the swing. "It's all yours, isn't it? The problem is yours, the solution is yours. I have to take that on trust, to believe that everything you do without explanation, each decision you make without my input, every question you don't answer and every kiss you give me without feeling anything for me, will somehow make life right for me and my baby."

She began walking back to the house, striding with a definition and purpose. He'd sent her away without explanation, without letting her in, too many times; now she was walking away without being sent. She was giving up on him, on any hope of sharing a life with him.

If she goes with Jimmy she'll never come back.

Reacting on instinct, he ran after her, grabbed her by the shoulder and hauled her into his arms, holding her close, leaning down to kiss her. Willing her to see what he couldn't say, to feel that he was giving her everything he had left…

She lifted her face to his, and for a moment he exulted in the sensuality he could draw from her with a touch; but then he saw the truth. The look in her eyes wasn't feminine arousal. Laila's face reflected the look he saw in his dreams every night in Jenny's dying face, and in the faces of the family he hadn't dared to visit since the funerals of his wife and daughter.

Utter betrayal.

"I'm not her," was all she said, simple, finite and damning. "I'll never be her."

Shame seared him, knowing what she thought, but his throat wouldn't work to tell her the truth. Every time he tried to tell her anything about Jenny and Annabel, the pain burst inside him until he thought his heart would stop.

"I know," he said, hearing his voice sounding like a rock on sandpaper. Suddenly realizing that she hadn't used his name once today.

The cracks between them were widening.

"Then don't use me. This is your baby, but I'm not your woman," she said quietly enough, but it was hard. She was hardening her heart against him.

"I deserved that," he muttered. His hands fell from her.

She nodded. "I don't belong to you."

When she walked away, the definition and decision were still there. She wasn't just walking away from this conversation. She was leaving.

Leaving him.

It came down to here and now. If he didn't force himself to tell her, if he couldn't find a way to reach her, he'd lose this last, amazing chance at life, love and happiness.

Until today, losing his child hadn't been an option. Now, he had to factor Laila into the most basic equation: Laila as a woman, as a person, with needs he could no longer overlook; but he had no idea how to give her what she needed from him without betraying Jenny and Annabel's trust, and breaking his sacred vow to them both.

The strangest sense of deep calm had overtaken Laila the moment she'd realized Jake would never stop loving the woman from his past. The depth of hopeless love only just realized, moments before it was lost: knowing she could have the man who held her heart in his grasp, without ever truly having him. Living a lifetime beside a man in chains, forever loving a soul too damaged to give her what she needed was all she'd ever have, and that could never be enough.

Laila walked through Marcie's lavender garden and reached the back veranda and opened the door without thinking, without preparing for the inquisition about to begin.

Glenn waited at the other side of the door. "Dar wants you, Lai," he said gently, and led her over to their father.

Like Glenn, Dar and Marcie both saw the look on her face, and softened. Marcie touched her face. "Jimmy and the boys stopped anyone following you out there."

Laila nodded, unable to speak.

Marcie drew her close. "He's a good man, Laila. A good friend to you."

Dar said quietly, "Yes, a very good friend." It was a statement, but the question lingered in his weathered face, in the eyes that blazed like an afternoon sky.

Laila couldn't answer what her father wanted to know. She'd never betray Jimmy's love for her.

She'd long known she was crazy to not love him back, but she loved him like she loved Glenn and Andrew, and all the wanting in the world couldn't make that change. Marrying Jimmy would only cheat and hurt a man who'd only given her love and support, and they both knew it.

That didn't mean she didn't hate the memory of Jimmy's pain when he'd guessed her pregnancy in a quiet, neutral tone, and knew nothing had changed for him when he offered to stand by her. He'd said his parents had started out on a similar footing, and they now had six kids and were very happy.

Saying no had been one of the hardest things she'd ever had to do.

Her gaze sought him out now, but he was already on his way over. His gaze was calm, his face without expression; he moved with a quiet dignity he rarely used in everyday life. When he reached her side, he held out his hand; she put hers into it, and ignoring the curious onlookers, he led her to the big, old-fashioned ballroom her grandfather had built forty-five years before.

The lively boot-scootin' music had just given way to something softer, mellower; lines had melted into couples.

Jimmy drew her close, but not too close. No claim made or accepted. She flowed into him, feeling warm and loved, grateful and sad.

"So you made your decision, huh," he said quietly, after a sudden dip that made her smile.

She nodded. "I'm sorry," she whispered.

"Nothing to apologize for," he whispered back. "It was always in the cards. You wouldn't have this little bun growing in your oven if you didn't feel strongly for him." He hugged her, making her feel warm and cherished. "I reckon you loved him from the start."

Laila's head drooped to his shoulder. "Doesn't matter what I feel, Jimmy. The point is, he doesn't love me. He never will."

"As my old granddad says, 'never' is too long to be sure of anything—and you're a pretty lovable character." He lifted her face, smiled down at her and kissed her forehead. "Just be yourself. Whatever's got him bound will untie itself in time."

When he spoke again, it was without anger or bitterness. "We're still mates, right?"

Fighting the urge to cry, she nodded. "I couldn't survive without you."

"Indispensable, that's me." He dipped her again, following her body until they seemed in danger of falling down. She laughed as he rectified the overbalance. "That's better. You haven't been laughing enough. Don't forget to be who you are," he intoned solemnly.

She laughed again, and hugged him.

"I've been watching him tonight," he went on, his eyes intent on hers. "He may not love you yet, but he can't leave you alone."

She shrugged. "That's the baby."

His brows lifted, even as he led her into another clumsy twirl. "Right. And that's why he's watching us now, with a face that tells me he doesn't know whether to kill me or you."

Frowning, she almost turned her head, but restrained

herself; she knew the thunder-look too well. Sick of repeating herself, she just shrugged. "I've given up trying to work him out."

Jimmy bent to her ear and said softly, "No man claims a woman and child as his own unless he wants them pretty badly—unless he has strong feelings about them both."

"May I cut in?"

He sounded like he'd swallowed gravel, yet still he was straining for politeness.

Laila turned her face from him. She wasn't ready to touch him, not now, while Jimmy's words were still taking effect. Believing Jake could have feelings for her would only make her weak, and she had to be strong, to be—

Jimmy's arm fell from her waist. "Be yourself, Your Worship," he whispered, and backed off.

Feeling unsteady, and almost unable to bear his arms around her, she felt the quivering begin when his firm hand touched her waist. She didn't look up for almost a minute. The rhythm had changed with his first touch, from warm and comfortable to a glorious pain: too much color and brightness. She had transformed from the warm darkness to cold light, and though it was beautiful, it was unbearably beautiful, as if the promise of heaven lay just beyond her grasp.

It was always that way with Jake.

Time seemed to dance with them as they moved together. He was all around her, within her, filling her with all that might have been, and what was, no matter how she longed to change it. When she was with Jake she was alive...

"You've made your point," he said quietly after a minute.

She looked up then. His face was as it had been the night she'd gone to him: white and ravaged. He was in the grip of excruciating darkness—yet his eyes weren't blinded now, but burning with purpose. Somehow she sensed he was fighting with all his strength to break free from what lay in his past.

Should she ask? Could she reach out yet again, only to find ridicule, rejection and hurt?

She drew a deep breath, to cleanse herself of the fears that were hurting them both, praying for the right words. "You took my family from me," she said finally, speaking right from the heart. "You made them your allies in your fears and wishes. I needed a friend."

Night covered his soul, darkening his face. "You're not stupid, Laila. He loves you."

"That's not your business," she said quietly. "His feelings are his own."

He gave a short nod. "True—unless you're planning to leave with him when he goes. Then it's *my* business."

She lifted her chin. "I wouldn't use him for my own ends. That's not what love is about."

His gaze lingered on her face for a moment before he answered. "But you wish you could. You're wondering if you're making a mistake."

Slowly she nodded. "I'm tired," was all she could think to say; but he nodded, and moved his fingers, a soft pull, asking without demanding. *Come to me.*

"Maybe it's time we pulled together?" he asked after a while, as if reading her mind.

Laila longed to run, but she found herself unable to do it. It seemed as if she'd just existed for so long, drifting through the days, deprived of the joy of living for so long—because until now he hadn't asked, or reached out from the heart.

Now she was seeing him, feeling him…

She took the step forward, moving into him, moving with him, around the floor in beauty and light. Unbearable sweetness, vibrant and strong. Jake and Laila together.

Rightness flooded her being. This story couldn't end any other way. How could she know nothing about him, and yet know that, somewhere deep inside, he needed her? The calling was inside her soul, from his to hers, imperative, undeniable, terrifying and enthralling her.

"Maybe it is," she said softly, but she knew he'd heard when his hand moved over the small of her back, not in sensuality but gentle…almost tender.

The sweetest pain she'd ever know. He seemed so close now, yet she knew she couldn't keep living like this, hoping, giving him what he needed while he held back all she must know about him to give him her trust, her life. Strength coursed through her.

"Did you dance with her like this? Was it like this when she touched you?" she blurted out, and didn't know if she said it because she wanted to hear it, or to break the unseen hold he commanded over her.

Or to force him to talk, to say something to her about his life.

Midway through the backward step he stumbled, pulling her with him. She gave an involuntary cry of pain as her back wrenched with the movement, making everyone look at them. He righted her quickly, but something snapped, like a current shut down. The life was gone from his face and body, leaving only the tautness of unspoken suffering, endless and unconquerable.

Suddenly, with the horrifying clarity that comes when blinders of jealousy and insecurity come off, she saw the truth. There could only be one reason for this bottomless well of grief. The woman he couldn't forget hadn't walked out on him, nor he on her.

The woman he loved was dead, and in her jealousy, she, Laila, had taunted him about it.

"I'm sorry," she cried. Stupid…why, *why* had she been so needlessly cruel?

"I know," he said quietly. "I know what you want, what you need, but I can't do it, Laila. I can't start a new life, act as if she never existed—" He covered his face with his hands. "I tried, for you, for the baby. I want to make you happy." He shuddered, and she felt sick with the pain she'd thrust back on him, when he'd been trying so hard to connect with her, to make things right. "*Don't ask again. Please.*"

Silent with shame, she nodded, knowing what he needed. "Go," she whispered.

He left the ballroom and the house in moments, his very private demons hounding him from behind.

CHAPTER EIGHT

"SHE looks much happier now," Andrew remarked to Jimmy as they stood shoulder to shoulder outside the stables a week later, watching Laila ride off on her pretty, lively Starfire, at a sedate pace, but riding. Old Blue loped along with the horse, barking at the stray sheep around the home paddock. Jake rode beside Laila on Red, the big gelding he'd brought with him to Wallaby Station.

Jimmy shaded his eyes with a hand against the late-morning sun, looking at her. "Yeah, she does." He smiled as Laila said something, and Jake nodded before they broke into a light canter, heading for the scrubby hills to the west. "My work here is done," he intoned in a mock-solemn voice that had the serious, quiet Andrew grinning.

"You did do it, you know. You made us all see what we were doing to her."

Jimmy shrugged, watching Jake's ease and grace in the saddle, compared to his lack of it with humans, especially Laila. "What friends are for…but it still might not work."

In the week since the party, Jake and Laila had done a polite dance of avoidance and brief greetings. Jake had only gone on the ride with Laila today when everyone, on Jimmy's instruction, had somewhere else they had to be. Jake couldn't bear for her to ride alone—and they all knew she'd go alone if she had to. She'd been denied the joy of riding for too long.

Jimmy and Andrew hid out in the back of the stables until Jake and Laila headed out. Jake wasn't stupid: if he saw them the setup he'd sensed would be confirmed.

The silence between the two men stretched out, until Jimmy said it first. "Reckon it's time for me to be heading back to Bathurst."

"You're welcome to stay," Andrew said, in all sincerity. "You're good for Laila."

"I was due back in lectures today, and practicals start Thursday." Jimmy turned to Laila's brother with a wry smile. "Besides, I make your Dar and Jake nervous. Probably everyone but Laila, but then she's used to how I feel about her."

The silence was uncomfortable for a few moments, before Andrew spoke, again in awkward sincerity. "She really does love you, you know."

"It's okay, Andrew," Jimmy said quietly. "Laila's put off life and love for my sake for long enough. Maybe if this works out, and she's unavailable, I might get out there as well."

He turned back to the house to pack his things, whistling as if he didn't have a care, but he was fooling no one, least of all himself. The whole Robbins family knew he loved Laila, just as his family knew.

This had probably been the hardest week of his life, but he'd done what he could to ensure Laila's happiness, as well as to give an unspoken farewell to his hopes of turning best friends to lovers, and winning the woman he'd loved for five years.

She'd have done the same for him: the push for happiness…and the goodbye.

Laila sighed. Even knowing it wouldn't last too long, she reveled in every moment she was on Starfire's back, with the stark and ochre-red Outback all around her in its busyness and its silence, and the pulsing of dry heat that lasted from mid-spring until late autumn.

"Every time I'm home, out here, I wonder how I could ever go back to Bathurst." She sighed. "I love my course, but the land just takes you somehow. It's like you don't belong to yourself anymore, but to this, to here."

"I went back home as soon as I'd done the course my dad expected of me," Jake agreed, frowning out over the hills and sunlight. "You can breathe out here."

She turned her head to look fully at him, then away: the yearning hurt her deep inside. When he was on a horse, it was almost more than she could bear. The fulfilment of every girlish dream she'd ever had was only four feet from her, the father of her child, who was probably wishing he was anywhere but here with her.

Blowing out a breath, she swung off Starfire and down to the ground. "I'll be back in ten minutes."

Jake was out of his saddle almost before she was. "Where are you going?"

She lifted a brow with a half smile. "Come on, Outback boy, do the math. It's been ninety minutes since we left. I'm five months pregnant, squashed in a saddle and I've been drinking all the water you push into my hand."

He grinned at her as he removed his hat, and wiped the sweat from his face. "A good reason to stay closer to the house from now on, maybe?"

She snorted inelegantly. "I'm a country girl, Connors. As if I care."

About to move away, she found herself held back by a firm hand. "Let me find a safe spot for you."

"Why?" she laughed at him, knowing her eyes must reflect her happiness that they were having something approaching a normal conversation, and that his touch didn't feel laden with the burdens of the past.

He lifted a brow. "You don't want to get comfortable on a

snake's burrow and provoke him into attacking you by flooding it, do you?"

She had to laugh again at the mental vision of that. "King, brown or tiger snake—it doesn't really matter. I'm fifty times their size—they're not going to fight me. Don't you do your Outback creatures research?"

He frowned at her. "Why would I? Australian snakes are the deadliest in the world."

Laila rolled her eyes. "Yeah, yeah, if we believe the results of tests performed on mice. And the poor snakes were provoked to attack because the researchers didn't feed them and then put their natural food right in front of them. Our snakes are very shy. You have to step right on one to make them bite—and any Outback boy should know that. Our snakes are mostly nonaggressive—and I'm wearing jeans and boots."

"A real country girl, prepared for anything," he mocked, but without malice. "What about green ants?"

"I promise to keep any exposed parts well out of the reach of any biting creatures." She moved out from under his hand, but loving the fact that he'd kept his contact with her without even thinking about it. "Now, unless you want me to embarrass both of us, stop arguing and let me get private."

He grinned again, and swept a hand toward the belt of trees just below the hill.

Her heart lighter than it had been for weeks, she made her way over the hill and down to the small line of scrub that would provide her with some privacy.

Strange that her admitting to something so embarrassing could make him lose the inner darkness that she knew hadn't always been his habit.

When she returned to the horses, Jake had spread a plastic-backed blanket over the hard grass beneath a scrubby tree, laid out two cellophane-wrapped sandwiches and a thermos with tin cups, and was sprawled beside the food with a grin. "I thought you might be hungry."

Laila could feel the slight double entendre there, the hidden invitation. Her body reacted to it, with the memories of midnight loving that were never far away; but responding to the lush sensuality between them only gave him an excuse to keep an emotional distance while he used it against her to maintain control. "What's on it?"

He chuckled. "I know about your aversion to meat. It's just tomato and lettuce. And the tea's herbal. Chamomile with peppermint and a touch of honey in case you get a queasy tummy."

She shook her head with a wry laugh as she flopped down beside him on the blanket, toughed by his sincerity. "You say that like I'm in kindergarten."

"At least I didn't give you Vegemite or peanut butter."

She grinned at his bantering tone. "Thanks for that…and for taking care of me."

He lifted a brow. "You mean you don't mind for once?"

"Pride and independence is useless when you're hungry and have a constantly hungry little someone inside you demanding to feed. I've been getting hungry all the time lately." She reached out for a sandwich, unwrapped it and dug in.

Jake unwrapped his sandwich, then poured the tea for her. "Just in case you need it."

"So solicitous," she teased between bites of the simple sandwich.

Smiling that gorgeous, crooked grin of his, he said, "See all the fun you've been missing out on?"

"Maybe you're worried you make bad sandwiches," she murmured in deliberate provocation. "The tea's your insurance in case you make me sick."

"I happen to make excellent sandwiches," he retorted. "I had to make them for Sandy and Aaron every day, growing up."

"But you made the tea just in case," she pointed out, wondering where his mother had been, what she'd been doing, but not willing to break the tentative connection they were making by asking the question. "You don't want me to make a mess of the blanket."

His eyes were warm and dark on her; the ghosts he dragged around behind him were nowhere in sight. "You got me."

They were flirting.

Laila's foolish heart began singing. The man lying less than three feet from her was the one she'd always sensed was lost somewhere inside him. He was reaching out to her…or maybe for once he'd forgotten the past that haunted his soul.

Knowing the connection between them was fragile at best, she chose to not push it, but laid down flat, looking up to the blazing sky, the tiny puffs of cloud chasing each other westward, and the galahs and cockatoos wheeling around overhead, screeching their lonely calls.

"It's so good to be outside again."

"I think you mentioned that before," he said, sounding lazy. Contented.

She twisted her face to give him a wry look. "So shoot me. I haven't had a lot of conversation lately."

"You've had plenty of conversation with your friend Jimmy…even one two hours away at the coffee shop."

A switch came into his voice, the silky tone of a man in dangerous waters. Laila's heart again rejoiced, hoping she wasn't the only one living in the grip of jealousy.

She decided to take the bigger risk and tell the truth, hopeful that he would follow and tell her things she needed to know. "Jimmy is one of only a handful of friends I made at Bathurst." She laced her fingers together over her belly, feeling her navel popping out with a little sigh. "Being the daughter of Brian Robbins is a shadow I never knew how to step out from. People wanted things—or thought things. I was never just Laila. Except with Danni—the friend I told you about—and Josie—

and Jimmy. One or two others, but we're not close, not the way I am with my friends. Especially Jimmy." She heard her voice soften with the name, but didn't look to see his reaction. "I met him the first year. He was my protector and savior. He became my study buddy, and he helped me get the job at the steak-house. He forced me out from studying and work. He dragged me to parties. He made me reach out to people. When everyone called me Princess Laila, he called me Your Worship, to make them all laugh, and realize there are nicer ways to tease someone."

"When did you know he was in love with you?" Jake asked quietly, without inflection.

"When he told me, about six months after my one and only romantic disaster." She sighed. "We tried, you know. We dated, held hands, kissed once or twice." She couldn't look at Jake as she said it; it felt too much as if she was betraying some-thing sacred. The gulp went down like a rock was lodged in her throat. "I wanted to feel what he did, to give him what he gave me, but it just wasn't there, and that hurt."

"Because you love him," Jake said, his voice gentle, reflec-tive. "Just not the way he wanted you to."

She sighed again, and nodded.

"If I hadn't taken responsibility for the baby, if I hadn't wanted to take care of you both, would you have married him? To feel less alone—just to feel loved and protected?"

The insight in his questions hit a core of pain in her soul— the whisperings of her conscience she hadn't even known was there until he voiced them aloud.

"Part of me wanted to, but I couldn't," she mumbled, feeling the flush cover her face. "I knew that would only have hurt him in the end."

The quiet wasn't uncomfortable, as she'd expected it to be. Time slipped by as they laid side by side, warm and windblown and content.

"You're a strong woman, Laila Robbins," he said after a while.

Uncomfortable with all he wasn't saying, she turned to him, resting her head on her hand. "He'll be a fantastic vet, you know," she added with a smile. "And a great dad, too. He's a fabulous big brother to the hordes back home. Some girl will be really lucky—" Her face broke out in a grin as the soft bubbles of movement rippled across her burgeoning belly. "The baby's saying hello." She took his hand in hers. "Want to feel him?"

Without his permission, she splayed his hand across her. "Hey, little one, this is your daddy. Want to say hi to him?"

After a very long forty-five second wait, she felt the tiny bumps quiver across where his hand rested.

Slowly a smile formed on his face until it seemed fair to split with the pride and joy. "Hi, little mate," he said, utter awe in his tone. "You wanted us to know you're listening in, huh?"

Laila smiled at him. "Better watch what we say. The doctor told me babies' ears develop pretty early."

His brows lifted as he kept his hand on her belly, running it over her with tender strokes to encourage the baby to move again. "It might have been good to tell me that the first day I knew about him."

There was no rancor in his tone, only a conspiratorial kind of humor, so she replied in kind. "Well, pardon me for being overwhelmed. You were a pretty scary proposition." She poked her tongue out at him, and wrinkled her nose.

His eyes darkened, but not in anger. "You have to be the most honest woman I've ever known, Laila." His gaze dropped to her mouth. "You don't play games." He leaned into her, obviously taking care not to hurt the baby. He hovered there, about two inches from her mouth, waiting for her signal.

"And you like that?" she whispered, her tone thick with the longing he could inspire in her so easily.

The answer was his mouth touching hers.

With a soft moan of joy she tangled her hands in his hair, bringing him closer, deepening the kiss. He made a rough sound in his throat as she opened her mouth for him, caressing her face and her hair. The kiss went on and on, but not in the frantic, needing passion she'd known first from him, or the calculating giving he'd shown her the past month or more.

Everything in the kiss and every touch was laden with tenderness. Laila's heart almost burst with the joy of it. She knew, oh, she knew that this time, Jake had no agenda but wanting to be with her, wanting to kiss her.

When his slow-drifting hand caressed her belly, the baby kicked against him, its first full, hard kick. Jake broke the kiss to laugh. "Do you think he's giving us a message?"

She smiled up at him. "I think he likes his mum and dad kissing."

He chuckled, and nuzzled her neck. "Do you mean him, or his mum?"

"Both," she whispered, flowing into his touch. "Oh, definitely both. Oh, *Jake*," she mumbled, reaching up to hold him where he nibbled at her shoulder.

"Yeah," he mumbled back, kissing along her shoulder and neck.

She arched up into his touch. "It's been so long…"

At her blatant sensual invitation, he lifted his head. His eyes smoldered, but held resolution, too. "We can't," he murmured, caressing her gently. "Not here. Not now."

"When?" she asked, filled with urgency. "When, Jake? I want you so much!"

He hushed her with a finger on her mouth. "We can't," he whispered in her ear, his body lying all the way alongside hers, close and warm and needing. "It's only been two weeks since the cramps. I won't put you and the baby at risk, no matter how much I want you."

She buried her face in his neck. "It won't hurt us. *This* hurts. Jake, I can hardly sleep. When you touch me, the feelings, the need, lasts for hours, sometimes days."

He gathered her close against him. "I'm glad to know it's not just me," he growled, his voice like rough gravel.

She shivered with yearning. "If I get Dr. Broughton's clearance…"

"Laila, I'm trying really hard to do the right thing here, and you're not helping much." He now sounded raw, burning with the same need blazing inside her. "The baby…"

"Is fine," she whispered, guiding his hand back to her belly. "See? There he goes again. He's telling you to make his mummy happy, Jake!"

Slow and soft, he kissed her. "Marry me, Laila. It will be so good for us."

Something clenched inside her. He was now offering a marriage with a shared bed. A small step for mankind—but a huge leap for Jake; and temptation clawed at her, heart and soul. If she married him and shared his bed, surely love couldn't be too far behind?

Every instinct screamed that this time, he wasn't manipulating her to get his way. She wasn't going to give in to that insecurity, not now, when being impulsive and emotional could change her entire future, and her baby's life. She uttered a brief, heartfelt prayer for guidance before she said the second set of words that had sprung up into her heart.

Touching his face, she looked deeply into his eyes, and took the risk. "If I say yes, will you invite your family to the wedding, Jake?"

His eyes closed. His face hardened, and she knew she'd lost him even before he spoke. "It's getting late." He got to his feet, and jerked his head toward the scrub below. "If you need to revisit over there, I'll pack up."

Laila held her tongue, knowing argument would get her

nowhere. At this point, she'd do far better to remember how far he'd come, rather than focusing on what she hadn't yet achieved.

In just over a month, he'd gone from offering a marriage of convenience to accepting they couldn't live anywhere near each other without aching to make love. He'd changed from coldness to teasing and kissing her as if he meant it.

Rome wasn't built in a day, Laila. Remember, all good things come to those who wait!

Yes, she had to work on her impatience; but that didn't mean that she couldn't continue to chip steadily away at his barriers.

She yawned delicately. "Good idea. I get more tired than usual lately."

He helped her to her feet, his coldness vanished in an instant, overwritten by concern. "Has this been too much for you?"

She smiled up at him. "I'm fine, Jake. The doctor says tiredness is normal at this stage of pregnancy, because of the baby's rapid growth. He said to continue a normal life, just sleep when I need to." She yawned again. The sleepiness had overtaken her with the first yawn, and now she couldn't stop.

In moments, she found herself up in his arms; then he laid her back down on the blanket, her hat placed over her face for extra shade. "Sleep now." His voice was rough with unspoken caring. "It's a long ride back."

Lying on her side, she wriggled around, trying to find a more comfortable spot, gave up and rolled up the side of the blanket beneath her belly while she only bent her legs slightly, instead of curling up as she used to sleep, prebaby. "The baby needs plenty of kicking space," she grumbled good-naturedly, "and if I don't give it to him, I don't rest. I don't know why he always has to begin his athletics career every time I'm relaxed."

Jake put his hand back over the baby. "Isn't he too little yet to hurt much?"

"Not this guy. He's made me aware of his presence in a very aggressive, *I'm going to be a forward in the football team* manner," she said, mock-aggrieved. "I think he's going to be a ten-pounder at least."

He laughed, sounding strained still—but Laila's heart bounced with happiness. "I think I was almost eleven pounds born, so it's likely."

"Did you play football, too?" she mumbled, sliding toward sleep.

"Sure did."

She nodded, and yawned again. "Thought so. I can imagine you ploughing through the opposition in your, *I'm here and don't bother with me* manner. Like father, like son…"

A soft chuckle. "I'd like to come with you on your next doctor's appointment, Laila."

Well past half asleep now, she groped for his hand, still resting on her belly from behind her, and pulled him down. "If you sleep with me now."

"Bargaining with me even when you're asleep. Impressive," Jake murmured as he lay down behind her, bringing his body in close to hers, and reveling in the rightness of lying with her this way. "Life with you will never be boring, Robbins."

But her even breathing told him she was already asleep. Softly, with a deep, abiding tenderness he would never show her while she was awake, he kissed her hair, and wished he could find the way to change his past and the person he was, so they could both find happiness; but that was impossible. So he kissed her again, and took what he could get: an hour of make-believe that when she knew all about him, she could somehow perform a miracle on him and he'd become the extraordinary kind of man with a clean, untainted past: the sort of man who'd really deserve her love.

CHAPTER NINE

NIGHT had almost fallen by the time they arrived back at the homestead.

Laila sat straight in the saddle, but her eyes were heavy, her face pale. Jake wanted to kick himself. He'd taken her too far from home for her first real ride in weeks. He should have followed his instincts and kept it local, a short half-hour ride followed by the picnic and a rest; but his guilt at restricting her for so long had let Laila dictate the pace.

Still, she'd slept for almost two hours, and he'd given her the softest spot and the rest of the blanket for the baby. He was itching where some bull ants had bitten him, lying on the tough grass beside her, waiting for her to wake up.

It had been the first time he'd laid beside her since the night they'd conceived the baby. It twisted his guts, remembering how good, how peaceful it felt to have Laila in his arms, scooped against his body, sweet and trusting in sleep, all barriers lowered.

He jumped from the saddle and flipped on the light when they reached the stables, then helped her down from Starfire. For once she didn't argue, but groaned and let her cheek flop onto his shoulder. "Thanks," she murmured. "The baby kicked almost all the way back. I feel like I've done three rounds with a heavyweight champion."

He chuckled and held her up, brushing her flyaway hair that seemed stuck to her face. "Let's face it, Laila, this kid doesn't have a hope of being quiet and still with us as parents."

She laughed, but it seemed dutiful. She was even more drained than she'd let on.

"Want help getting to the house?" He moved to turn her toward the house.

Shaking her head, she stepped back. "I've got to get Starfire comfortable first."

"I'll do that for you. Just for tonight," he added with a grin, seeing her eyes flare with resentment. "It was your first ride in weeks, we went too far, your sleep wasn't comfortable and the baby's kicking exhausted you. You have to be balanced about this, Laila. Meet me halfway."

After a moment, she nodded. "All right. I'd appreciate it." She looked up at him, the uncertainty clear to read in her dark sky gaze. "What are we doing, Jake?" she whispered. "Are— are we friends now?"

He resisted the urge to deny it with all the hot rebellion rising in his soul. "Maybe we have more in common than I'd thought at first," he said, with caution. He didn't want to make any promises he couldn't keep.

A tiny smile tugged at the corners of her mouth. "I'm glad. Maybe it's what we should have been all along." She yawned, and therefore missed the brief hardness that crossed his face.

He knew he ought to agree; for the baby's sake, for Laila's sake, too, since it seemed she didn't have all that many true friends away from Wallaby…but it wasn't going to happen, not while he wanted her so much he ached day and night with it. He had a bad feeling that this particular ache was one that couldn't even be cut surgically from his system.

How on earth had Jimmy loved Laila so many years, lived close to her and repressed it? As soon as he'd had a taste of her, his days and nights had been filled with craving for more.

He started when he felt the soft brushing of lips over his cheek. "Thank you for a lovely afternoon. I think I'll be able to sleep tonight, despite what I said earlier."

Her eyes twinkled; a soft blush touched her cheek. She'd just mirrored everything he was thinking. She still wanted him—badly, if her reaction to his kiss today was anything to go by…and her words.

Was she letting him know that she'd take what he was willing to give?

Parents who couldn't stay together eventually became friends; it happened all the time. He'd been friends with Jen first, before love came along quietly, natural and sweet; then urgency had come for them in its time. But he couldn't even think of Laila without burning for her. The urgency was always there, the wanting and need, and he had a feeling it would last a lifetime.

Pain slashed across him, but it was more like whacking a scar than tearing at an open wound…even the guilt at the thought hurt less—but he didn't want to forget. *Never*.

"You need the rest, with this little guy." He rubbed her belly; but instead of fatherly tenderness, he felt the forbidden fire streak through every nerve ending. *Touching Laila*. "Go," he said, his voice strangled.

The light in her eyes dimmed. She turned and walked out of the stables, holding the small of her back with one hand.

Resisting the urge to follow her, to massage her obvious discomfort away, he turned back to the horses and unsaddled them, hung up the saddles, blankets and bridles and prepared to currycomb them before he went in for dinner.

"I want to talk with you." Brian Robbins's voice came from right behind him.

His boss didn't sound belligerent, just determined. Jake suppressed a sigh. "Of course, sir." He put down the brush and soapy water bucket and turned to the man who'd given him a place to hide from the past the last year. "What can I do for you?"

Robbins's weatherbeaten face held the same determination as his voice. His hands splayed across his hips. "I've tried to be patient with you, to let you do the right thing in your time, but I want to know when you're going to tell my girl the truth about who you are. I want to know when you'll take her home to Burrabilla to meet your family."

The shock raced along every nerve ending to his fingertips. Suspecting Laila's father knew the truth was one thing; hearing the name of his home on the older man's lips made him fling up a hand in instinctive denial. "Sir—"

"Don't. I knew your father. You look more like your mother, but the Sutherland stamp is unmistakable." Robbins swatted Jake's hand until he allowed it to fall. "I've known you were the missing Sutherland heir since you started here. I've minded my own business, even when you got my girl pregnant and still didn't tell her. I gave you time to get her to come to your way of thinking. She's a strong-minded girl, my Laila."

"You've got that right," Jake muttered, pulling off his hat and twirling it on his finger. He hesitated a moment, then asked, "Does she know anything about me?"

"Are you asking if she's heard the gossip concerning the deaths of your wife and daughter?" Robbins asked, his voice rough with unspoken sympathy. "Not through us—but apart from that, I couldn't tell you. We're a long way from Burrabilla and the Outback's a big place. What's more, she spent most of her time on school breaks doing what work experience she could get. If she knows, she hasn't shared it with us."

Jake had wheeled away with the first mention of his past. "You knew, and let me stay here?" he asked, his voice strangled.

Brian's gaze was puzzled. "You thought I'd drive you out of here, away from Laila and your own child, because of a tragic accident?"

Jake's shoulders slumped. He couldn't speak; it was all he

could do to stop the tears burning his eyes at a hundred and eighty degrees.

The gentle hand on his shoulder startled him. "Son, I think you've suffered enough for one lifetime. Shed the weight, boy. Tell Laila, and see what she says."

All Jake could do was shake his head. He knew what his feisty, giving Laila would say...and until he could feel he deserved that redemption, he couldn't reach out. No matter if he was dying inside a little more every day without her...

"Jake—is that what you're really called?"

Jake nodded. "My dad was John. Jacob is my middle name." His voice was husky.

"Okay, then. Jake." The hand on his shoulder tightened a little. "Jake, have you always been this unforgiving to yourself? Or do you apply higher standards to yourself than to the rest of the human race? No wonder your kindness to Laila always comes out a little on the tough side."

Frowning, Jake muttered, "You don't understand."

"Son, my first wife died because we were far from help when she had an accident. Who can understand better?"

Brian's voice was restrained, tight, and still, despite his happiness with Marcie, held love for his long-dead wife as he spoke.

"Minette's been gone twenty-one years this March, and I still hurt—I still remember. So I do understand, Jake...and Marcie understands and appreciates that. There's nothing to say Laila won't understand if you tell her. It might help your situation."

Jake turned his head to face Brian. "Why?"

Brian made a rueful face. "She's not stupid, you know—far from it. She knows something is driving you to act the way you do, but it's hurting her. I know you want her trust—but why should she trust you with her future, when you won't trust her with your past?"

Jake almost choked as a ball of pain came burning up from his chest.

"Think about it," Brian said, very quiet and serious. "It took me a long time, too—but when you do, the results could surprise you. It might be better than you think."

All Jake could do was shake his head. How could things ever get better? How could he *let* things get better? To do so was to betray Jenny and Annabel's memory.

Brian sighed. "When you're as old as me, you'll know that finding love again doesn't discount the love you knew before— and living in apology won't bring them back. Refusing to live does nothing for them but discredit what you had. I know that, too."

The pain in his throat was like a band constricting him from speech; the knot in his gut just twisted tighter and tighter...and Brian just stood there, waiting. Finally he said the only thing that came to mind. "I have to get the horses done."

A tired sigh came from behind him. The hand fell from his shoulder. "It won't bring them back, son," Brian said quietly, and left the stables; and Jake turned back to Starfire's flanks, brushing down by rote. The action soothed him, its familiarity, but he didn't see the animal. He didn't see Jenny's lovely face smiling at him, either, or even in her final hour of agony.

All he could see was the two graves he hadn't visited since the funerals.

Laila sighed and rolled over again. 2:14 a.m. and she hadn't slept more than half an hour.

The discomfort from the baby's stretching left her restless, unable to find that deep, refreshing sleep she'd once fallen into with little trouble. She wandered in and out of vivid dreams that meant nothing, but left her disoriented and on edge.

Stupid just lying here, with this useless sense of waiting for something to happen...and she was hungry anyway.

She tossed off the covers—the nights were turning cool from hot days, as only Outback nights could do. Pulling on a terry robe, she padded downstairs to the kitchen.

The bananas were green, as were the apples, and she only liked red ones. Sighing, she headed for the fridge to pour a glass of milk.

A soft voice echoed across the big, empty kitchen. "You okay, darling?"

Laila turned to her stepmother, smiling. "I woke up hungry." She held up her glass.

"That's not enough. Nighttime hungries mean you need protein—water if you're not pregnant." Marcie bustled over to the fridge and pulled out two eggs. "Scrambled?"

Laila shuddered as she sat at the scratched kitchen table. "Sorry, Marcie, the thought of butter."

Marcie smiled at her, and got out a saucepan instead. "Poached, then—you can't get blander than that." She set about cooking.

Knowing this was Marcie's domain, Laila didn't try to stop her. As the youngest child, she had become Marcie's daughter too many years ago. She would have called her Mum, but for Dar's pain when she'd tried. When eleven-year-old Laila had shed tears of distress, Marcie had taken her upstairs to her room, and gently explained that though Dar loved her, he hadn't forgotten Laila's real mother, either. "Though you call me Marcie, I'll know you mean Mum," she'd whispered, smiling and kissing her tenderly.

She was shaken out of her reverie by a plate being set before her at the table. "Eat, sweetie—and when you're done, maybe you can tell me what's bothering you."

Laila shot Marcie a grateful look. "Thank you. Maybe I will." She chewed her food slowly, unsure if it would help or give her indigestion. Everything pretty much seemed to do that these days.

Through the west-facing French doors behind the table, in the half-moon's gentle but clear light, something moved.

Laila frowned and narrowed her eyes to focus, wishing she'd brought down her study glasses. Usually the night was still out here, only trees swaying if there was a breeze. Of course, it could be a kangaroo, but she thought it looked human.

The movement came again, coming closer. It wasn't frightening, but Laila's awareness grew with every movement; the sense of waiting for something crystalized. He turned a little, just into the light, and she could feel him there, watching over her and the baby.

Marcie stood behind her chair. "It's him," she said softly, confirming her heart's belief. "I've seen him before at night. He doesn't seem to sleep much."

She could hear the smile in Marcie's voice, but Laila couldn't tear her gaze from the shadowy figure. Why was he watching the light without coming in? Surely from where he stood he could see her clearly…

As if compelled beyond her will and reason, she pushed her chair back, opened the doors and walked out to him.

Barefoot, the cool night breeze washed over her feet and legs; the moonlight, filtered through the windbreaker ghost gums, was eerie and cold. She shivered, and shivered again, but kept moving toward where he watched her and waited.

When she reached him, he pulled off his jacket and put it around her shoulders without saying a word, while Laila tried to find the right words to say.

"You'll be cold," she whispered.

He shrugged. "It doesn't matter."

It does to me.

But he wouldn't accept words of caring from her. Why was it that everything she wanted to say seemed taboo?

Finally she gave up and blurted out the wrong words. "Do you always watch the house—watch over me—at night?"

"I don't sleep much. Two, maybe three hours." Another shrug, as if that, too, didn't matter.

"Why? Do you feel the need to protect us night and day?"

His jaw hardened, but eventually, when she waited in silence, he inclined his head.

"Jimmy left tonight," she said quietly, not knowing why.

"I saw."

She whispered, looking up into that face as beautiful and cold as the night, "Will you ever tell me why, Jake?"

They both knew she wasn't talking about Jimmy's departure.

"Have you talked to your father tonight?"

Surprised by the tautness of his voice, she tilted her head, in obvious enquiry, but he didn't say more. She knew he wouldn't.

"Good night." She turned to the house. "Go back to your room. I'm fine, apart from being hungry."

"Laila." His voice was commanding.

She shook her head. "Don't, Jake. Whatever it is, I'm too tired to hear it." She took a step, two, then remembered his jacket, and peeled it off.

He caught the jacket as she threw it. "Laila, we need to talk."

Shaking now with a fury she hadn't known she was capable of, she wheeled back. "Oh, so now he wants to talk? Are you going to talk, or is it all up to me, as usual? Am I expected to give all of myself, while you give nothing?"

He stood very still and quiet. Just watching her.

"How unusual," she mocked under her breath. "I'm tired of doing all the talking."

"Laila." The word seemed grated out of his throat. "Can't you see I'm trying here?"

"Yes—but for every step forward you take, you end up taking another two backward." Her eyes were burning. She rubbed at her cheek with a fist she only knew was clenched at that moment. "Waiting for you to see me is like waiting for the drought to break."

His eyes blazed. "I see you."

When she blinked hard, she felt the tears fall in tiny drips. "Then why do I *feel* invisible? Why is it that whenever you look at me, I think you're wishing she was alive, and you were with her instead of me?"

In the white-and-gray light he should have seemed godlike,

carved from marble—that was the way she'd always seen him—but this night, this moment, all she saw was the man: a man trying so hard to break free from his self-imposed prison, but no longer knowing how he'd built it. A man lost in a maze of old choices, old loves—of *memory*.

Her gaze fell from his face, before love and compassion entwined so intricately she would be in a prison of her own. "I can't wait for you anymore."

He lifted a hand to her in silent plea. "Laila." His voice cracked.

She shook her head. "I can't." And she turned toward the house, her heart pounding so hard, aching so much, she almost couldn't breathe.

"I need you."

Laila halted midstep at the voice: the voice of the night she'd gone to him—the stark yearning she hadn't heard in his voice in months. Her eyes closed over; a gasp of air from lungs suddenly unfrozen hurt her. Oh, how she ached and burned to answer his call. *He needs me.*

A tiny whisper came from somewhere deep inside, from everything that made her a woman. "I can't keep hoping, can't keep waiting for you, risking it all and getting nothing, always shut out of your life. It's over."

"Laila! Laila, *no*! Wait!"

She shook her head, and strode toward the house.

Within moments he'd caught up to her, and he swung her around to face him, holding her up. "It's not over," he snarled, his hands holding her against him. His face was so close that everything but his eyes was a blur, but his intensity zapped through her like a surging current. "It'll never be over. Damn it, you woke me up from a five-year sleep, made me ache and hunger and want. You can't walk away now. I won't let you!"

His mouth crashed down on hers with the final word—but Laila refused to respond, no matter how badly she hungered to give in.

This moment—everything he'd said—was too important to let him distract her now.

She struggled against him until he let her go. "You've woken up? You want something from me besides the baby? Prove it," she cried. "I can find a guy at the local pub to kiss me if I want. I could get half a dozen guys around here to marry me if marriage was all I was after. Give me a reason why I should choose you!"

Standoff. His shutters crashed down as his mouth had on hers moments before. His body, stiff and cold and half-averted, screamed his rejection louder than any words could.

Aching, she wanted nothing more than to curl in a ball and cry him right out of her life—but he'd *never* let her go, not with their child binding them. She lifted her chin and looked into his eyes, just as cold. "Check and mate. Don't bother me again until the baby's born. You have rights to him, but none to me. *None*."

And she turned for the house once more.

"Laila!" An imperative call came from the house. Marcie. "Laila, come quickly!"

Imagining she'd fallen and hurt herself, Laila bolted homeward. "Marcie? Marcie, are you okay?" she cried as she raced through the double French doors.

"I'm fine," her stepmother panted, looking frazzled—not a state the unflappable Marcie was often in. "The Appleyards' prize mare's foaling, and the foal is breech. Nothing they've tried has worked, she's bleeding and Dave Randall's already on an urgent call to the Brenners. They desperately need help." Marcie gave her a swift, uncertain look. "They've asked for you."

About to bolt upstairs, she stopped and turned back. "Marcie, they're aware I can only help in an unofficial capacity? I'm not qualified, and if I help, it's at their own risk?"

Marcie nodded. "Did you think I wouldn't protect you, sweetie? They know the risks. You're there to help out, not as a qualified vet—and they're sending a fax as we speak to that effect, signed by both Appleyards."

"Tell them I'm on my way, then." Elated and unsure at once, she strode past Marcie to her room. "I'll get dressed. Get my kit out, will you, and the silken ropes and the birthing harness—and call one of the boys to pack the light plane with my gear and have it ready for takeoff. Ask the Appleyards to have the airstrip clear."

A deep voice, one laced with fear yet reassurance, came from the direction of the French doors. "I'll fly you there. Don't worry about her, Marcie, I'll be with her the whole time."

"Why am I not surprised about that?" she muttered. Since someone had to fly her there, she didn't answer, just passed through the door to the stairway.

Four Tree Run, Outback New South Wales

"Come on, little one, please," Laila was begging the orphaned foal that was refusing to drink the milk from a mare rubbed over with her dead mother's skin. "Please, baby, just drink. Your mother would want you to live, sweetheart, please!"

Weak, standing on shaking legs, the foal had turned her head from the mare's offered sustenance, after Laila had once again rubbed the teat with the mare's skin.

The unreality of the situation the night before had long since turned grim. Walking through the cool, starlit night and through the big, wooden double doors to the warmth of a fire and quiet, dim-lit darkness and people hunched over something lying in the hay in the middle of the stables, it almost looked like a divinity play to Jake.

Then Laila strode in and took over, and the image shattered—the reality was blood and mess and snapped orders, and he'd accepted the role of assistant.

But she couldn't stanch the bleeding; no medicine currently known to veterinary science could stop the inevitable. Yet with blood on her hands and tears streaking her white face, Laila had kept going, trying delivery by rope, sedating the mare into unconsciousness first—but it had been obvious to Jake from the first glance that this birth was far from divine.

The mare was always going to die, and she did, at 5:00 a.m. Laila had finally taken the shotgun and ended the mare's suffering, refusing to let him or anyone else take on the grim task.

It was midday now. The bell for the meal had been sounded ten minutes before. Jake knew better than to try to make Laila go into the dining room for lunch. Watching her work through the night and morning, he realized something about the woman he had seduced, bullied, cajoled, pushed, prodded and guilt-tripped in his determination to make her his.

Laila was destined for far greater things than to be the wife of a nameless jackaroo.

Her skills had him in awe. Her emotions didn't get in the way of her job, they enhanced it. She didn't give up when he, a one-time breeder, would have called it natural attrition and let the foal die. She'd forced pumped milk down its throat, made it swallow, tried to give it a taste of life—a life it didn't want.

Why did that sound familiar?

He shook his head and made his way to the kitchen of the homestead to get two plates for them, as he'd done this morning for breakfast, and for the cups of tea Lena Appleyard had brought out. No way would he leave Laila. She was beyond exhaustion—but at least she wouldn't be cramping. He was glad he'd thought to ask Marcie to pack Laila's tablets.

She'd taken one without thought this morning when he'd handed her the water and pill.

"Thanks," she'd said briefly, barely knowing who he was, then thrust the empty glass back in his hand and continued treating the foal.

She'd slept for about twenty minutes—the most she'd take—at 6:00 a.m., while he kept up the force-feeding and cajoling the foal. She'd laid on a bed of hay covered with a horse blanket, turning to ice when he'd tried to talk her into finding a sofa or a bed inside. "Do I tell you how to do your job?"

He couldn't argue with that. She didn't need his advice. She was a damn fine vet.

And deserved her chance to finish her degree and start her own practice.

He had to face facts. Just because he didn't deserve to get on with living life to the full, it didn't give him the right to drag Laila down with him.

Jake felt the decision coming at him like a fast train hurtling down the track toward him. The life change he'd refused to even contemplate for five years was imminent, no matter how he tried to remain deaf and dumb to it.

He blanked out the thought, grabbed the plates of food with a murmur of thanks and headed back to Laila; but when he returned to the warm, deliberately darkened stables, he heard the soft sound he'd learned to dread.

He dropped the plates without thought and ran to her. Seeing her hunched over herself, rocking back and forth while she sobbed, he felt his chest constrict, then explode.

He scooped her up in his arms and held her close as she cried. Feeling the rightness of her inside of him, part of him, without thinking about it. "I'm sorry, Laila, I'm so sorry. You did all you could—"

But Laila shook her head. "She's drinking," she whispered against his cheek.

He turned his head, and saw that it was true. Weak suckles at best, but the foal was drinking from the mare.

Hesitant to burst her bubble, he tried to find a tactful way to say what he needed to.

"I know," she murmured, her breath stirring against his cheek. "Without her mother, she probably won't make it, especially since she's a racing breeder, not a stock horse."

Perversely, hearing her say it fired up his arguments from the other side. "Fostering can work. Back home, we had no less than six breeding foals that made it after we lost the mare, and they went on to—" Then, realizing what he was saying, he clamped his mouth shut.

Laila stiffened, and jerked out of his lap. "I have to apologize to Ron for the mare. *No,*" she said when he made to follow her. "I'm not a child. I don't *need* your strength. So make yourself useful, and get the plane ready. I want to go home."

If Jake could kick his own butt, he'd have done it right then. Why did he wreck it every time Laila was starting to trust him? It was as if he was deliberately sabotaging himself—

He blinked, frowned and shook his head and, before his mind could take over again and wander into dangerous emotional territory, got to his feet and headed for the house to thank the Appleyards before readying the plane.

Two hours of silence from Laila left Jake feeling more unnerved—and more talkative—than he'd been in five years.

The look haunted him still.

Returning from the primed plane, he saw two men with Laila: one was Tom Appleyard, the other a stranger...possibly Dave Randall, the veterinary surgeon he'd called himself over an hour before. Laila's head was lowered, one hand half-lifted.

"Even if I could have come in time, the mare would have died anyway. The blood loss all but guaranteed it. I told Tom at the start that she was a racer, but not the best for breeding," he added, with a pointed glance at the old-school ringer and new player in the racing stakes.

Laila's ponytail slipped over one shoulder as she shook her head. "No, I should have done more—I don't know, *something.*"

Tom Appleyard muttered something—and obviously Laila agreed with that, because she nodded, slow and unutterably weary. "I know. I'm sorry, Tom. You don't know how sorry."

Jake strode over to give support whether Laila wanted it or not. "This can be sorted out later. Laila needs rest. She's been up all night working on the mare and foal. She *is* pregnant, remember," he added with slight emphasis—enough to make Tom shift on his feet and give an uncomfortable glance at Laila's hand, rubbing her rounded belly.

"Thanks for coming, Laila," Appleyard said awkwardly. "You saved the foal, which is more than I'd have been able to do." But it was clear he'd expected Laila to pull a rabbit out of a hat—or a miracle out of her bag of tricks—and was still disappointed in her.

He supposed the stubborn old coot needed someone to blame for his stubbornness and stupidity in not calling sooner, and Laila wasn't arguing.

That struck him with unexpected force. *Laila wasn't arguing*. His feisty earth angel, strong and wise, had nothing to say for once…but the sudden look she gave him was the one haunting him still, as he was about to descend onto the Wallaby airstrip.

The silent, almost blinded desperation. *Please get me out of here…*

She didn't resist as Jake took her hand and led her to the plane—she'd just wandered along with him, climbed into the plane when he told her to, clicked her belt in place and sat there. Unseeing eyes staring out the window. Fingers sitting quiet and obedient in her lap.

He'd tried everything he could think to say—he'd even tried to provoke her into a fight by ordering her to bed as soon as they reached Wallaby; but there was no response, not even a shift in her breathing. She'd gone to a place inside herself where he couldn't follow, and he didn't know if she wasn't letting him in, or if she didn't even know he was with her.

"Descending into Wallaby," he all but snapped, as tired as she was and filled with a resentment that wouldn't fade. Why wouldn't she talk to him? "No doubt the family will be waiting to hear all about your triumph today."

Checking her with a swift glance, he couldn't tell if she'd given any response; but—no, something had changed and he'd missed it. The blinded look was still there, but she seemed—trapped, somehow...like a poor, slow old wombat trying to cross a highway with a road train bearing down on it, seeing the inevitable but unable to change it.

The hunted deer look. Stricken and terrified and helpless...and still she didn't fight.

"It was a triumph today, Laila," he said, driven to exempt her from blame. "You saved the foal's life. Nobody could have saved the mare, but the foal—"

"Please."

She didn't say any more, but she didn't have to. The one word shouldered a burden of guilt and carried a cartload of shame, and it silenced him.

He'd been shouldering that burden and pushing that cart around for years.

He landed the plane, and moved it into the big old shed they used as a hangar, wishing he knew what to say, what to do to make this better for her.

Laila opened her side of the plane and hit the ground running, her passivity gone in an instant. With the awkward gait of growing pregnancy she headed straight for the house, without an instant's pause or even a *thank-you-for-all-your-support-today, Jake.*

He stalked after her, hard and fast, feeling overlooked, treated as if all he'd done for her wasn't enough...as if he was—invisible...

Laila bolted through the door as if she couldn't get away from him fast enough—but no way was he leaving it like this. If she could tell her family, tell Jimmy her secrets, she could talk to the man she was going to marry—

There were too many echoes in his head, in this place…in
Laila's words. Too many echoes of the past in everything she
did and said, rising up to accuse him. This place, this woman,
was haunting him as much as home.

No! He tore up the stairs and opened the screen door before
he could give in to the screaming need inside him to turn and
run, to be alone and safe again in his solitude.

She was almost up the stairs to the second floor by the time
he reached the open living area, with Joe, Marcie and Glenn
all frightened, anxious and about to tear up after her.

He stopped about ten feet behind them, lost in her face. The
tears. The suffering. The blame and self-hate. The silent pleading as she looked at him—only at him.

Pushing past Glenn, he ran up to her. Seeing her eyes
drenched in desperate yearning for a redemption she didn't
believe she'd find, the panting breaths and terrible, unbearable
need, he pulled her close, then lifted her into his arms and
carried her to her room.

No one could understand a need for sanctuary more than
he…and he'd give it to her, even though he could feel that train
of inevitability hurtling at him at a thousand miles an hour.

CHAPTER TEN

LAILA felt the familiar comfort of her cushion-top bed envelop her, her comforter cover her; but she couldn't sigh and roll into sleep. Her mind kept rolling the film of the past sixteen hours, rewinding and replaying it over and over, as she searched for the clue she'd overlooked, the one tiny clue to what happened that she'd dismissed as unimportant.

If she couldn't find it, the mare's life would be lost for no purpose.

Seven years of training had meant little, faced with reality; beneath the pressure of life and death, she'd lost every technique taught to her.

With the mare's death, she'd seen her lifetime's ambition turned to dust and ashes before her eyes. Her life, her sense of self-worth, for years had been wrapped up in this one investment: that she'd be a good...no, a *great* vet. She'd wanted to save animals for as long as she could remember. She still remembered the time when she'd brought home the funnel web spider and Dar took her to the hospital, convinced she must be dying of a bite.

"Let it out, Laila. The family won't come in, not while I'm here."

The voice, the words snapped off the stupid, irrelevant memories, yet somehow soothed the turbulence inside her. He understood. How could she face them after her failure today?

"You won't find it, you know," he said quietly. "There's no rhyme or reason, and nothing you missed. It was too late by the time we got there. It would have taken a miracle to save her."

Why did that absolution seem to come to her mind as if across a universe of time, slow and distorted? Her anguished heart craved the balm, yet it reached her like a cold echo of truth. She couldn't make her mouth open; her tongue cleaved to her mouth, refusing to work.

Her first call out shouldn't end like this!

The bed dipped and swayed as he sat beside her, then lay down, taking her in his arms to halt the shivers with his warmth. "I know, baby, I know," he mumbled, kissing her hair. "It means so much, and you're an amazing vet. But you can't perform miracles, Laila, no matter how much you want to. She was dying before we got there. You kept fighting for her long after a lot of people would have put her down."

Couldn't he see that was the problem? Her every dream, every thought of her first call out was of saving a creature in distress—but all she did was to add to the suffering of the poor mare, because she hadn't been good enough…because she'd refused to let her go.

She couldn't take the comfort he offered. Though she'd never felt such tenderness from him, she remained stiff and un-yielding in his arms.

After long moments lying entwined in silence, together skin to skin yet never further apart, he whispered, "You had me in awe today, you know that? The way you fought for the mare and foal. You saved one when I was sure neither could be saved."

From deep inside, a screaming protest tore out of her soul, yet when the words came, they were soft and sad. "You don't understand."

She felt the tiniest relaxing of his body, and realized how

tense he'd been until she spoke. "I don't think anyone could understand where you're at right now better than I do," he muttered, low yet harsh with a strange relief.

Why? After all these months, did this mean he finally cared about how she felt?

All she could do was to shake her head. Now it seemed the words were her driving force, and she couldn't stop them if she wanted to. "I failed. The mare died—the foal lost her mother—because I wasn't good enough." She gulped, but the rock-hard pain in her throat refused to shift. "What makes me think I can look after my baby? I don't know a thing about babies—"

"Whoa, whoa." Startled by her leap in logic, Jake laid a finger across her lips. "Laila, you'll make yourself sick. This can't be good for the baby."

Her head lifted; wild-eyed, she stared at him. And then, slow and sort of crazy, she laughed. "See? I'm a bad mother already."

"No. No, you're not. Laila, stop this!" He grasped her by her shoulders, not shaking her, but holding with a grip she couldn't pull away from. "There's no connection between losing the mare and your ability to raise the baby." He sighed, wishing he knew the right words, *any* words, to help her. "I realize you're hurting right now, but try to get this in perspective. It was a mare. Prize livestock, yes, but still livestock. You're an Outback woman. You know the statistics. The cycle of nature out here is that we'll lose between eight to fifteen percent of stock. Appleyard was a fool to bring a racing mare out here and breed her against advice."

Wrong words, obviously. She just shook her head.

"Don't let this affect your confidence, Laila. You're going to be an amazing vet. You need to get back up on the—bike," he said, after almost saying *horse*. "Don't give up after only one—" *Failure? Loss?*

It still wasn't working. She lay passive in his arms, feeling like a rag doll. Lost in self-blame, torturing herself for a tragedy that was always going to happen—

You can't blame yourself, Jake. Jenny was beyond help. It was too early for the baby.

You know Jen, always stubborn. We all told her to take it easy...

She would want you to get on with life!

In a shock too profound for words, Jake watched her...and saw through a warped mirror to the man he'd been five years ago. A man fallen so far down the loss and blame spiral he couldn't see the hands reaching out to him, the stumbling words of redemption, the loving friends and family trying to heal him.

He hadn't believed in redemption then. Five years later, he still didn't believe he deserved it, or the love and healing people held out to him, from his anxious family to the mighty, loving Robbins clan. So how was it now that he found himself repeating the words his family and friends had said to him five years before?

She'd reached out to him. Somehow she knew, must know that he understood; that his past was the key to her own healing.

So do it. Tell her. Tell her the truth.

All the lights went out inside him, leaving him shivering and cold. The only connection he had to life and warmth was the woman beside him, the woman who'd risked her pride and heart over and over to reach him, to heal him—the woman whose entire life had changed, and not for the better, by meeting him. The woman who now seemed as lost as he'd felt during these past five years.

She didn't deserve this suffering. If it was allowed to continue, it would stain her self-confidence as a vet, if not as a mother. She wouldn't even be here at Wallaby now if he'd used protection that night, instead of thinking only of his own pain and his comfort.

He had to help her.

Without thinking about it, he reached backward to turn off the lamp, and the soft glow of a gathering dusk filled the room with intimacy, an illusion of privacy and *safety*. He closed his eyes and tried to breathe; but he could only draw in the basics to stay alive as he blurted the words he'd held in for too many years.

"Her name was Jenny. She was my wife, and pregnant with our daughter, Annabel."

Laila had become completely still. He didn't need to open his eyes, though: he could feel her coming to life, just by hearing her breathing change. She was listening. She was open to him, and not about to interrupt with unnecessary questions on who *she* was.

"When she had eight weeks to go before the birth, it was muster. Burrabilla is a working cattle property with over two thousand head of good Poll Herefords. I had to get the yearlings to sale—it was my responsibility, but I could see Jenny wasn't comfortable—she'd barely slept the night before, and she held her back as she walked. She wanted the nursery painted pink, with baby mobiles and a little-girl border put under the picture rails. I told her I'd do it after muster was done." He shrugged, and dragged in a quick breath of air before expelling it. "I should have seen her pain, and stayed home with her."

She didn't move, just breathed in, breathed out. Waiting.

So he kept talking, forcing the words out. He told the whole story, at first because it would help Laila; but as he spoke, the pressure of the darkness living inside him, heavier from being mute for so long, felt like a coil releasing.

Finally, after the dusk symphony of chirping crickets and screeching galahs gave way to the soft chirruping hiccup of small parrots finding roost for the evening, he opened his eyes, looked at Laila and finished his story. "So I left Burrabilla, and John Jacob Sutherland, behind. I became Jake Connors, jackaroo. I worked at four other stations, each one further south from home, until I came here. If somebody started to wonder about me, or got too close, I'd leave the place. Until I came here," he repeated, wondering why he did so.

But he was done. He'd said it all, and sweet, blessed relief filled him. The pain of silence, feeding upon itself, had grown into a black malignant cloud through the years, taking him over. Just telling someone, telling Laila, lightened the burden...

What was she thinking?

"So Jenny agreed not to decorate the nursery until you came back?" she finally asked, her tone thoughtful.

"She said she'd only paint the bottom half of the room," he said slowly. "I didn't even like that, but I knew her. She liked the Outback life, was raised to it, but she didn't like being alone doing nothing." He smiled at her. "You and Jen were alike that way, both very active people. She had to keep busy while I was gone. So I agreed."

"So you knew she'd keep going when that was done?"

"I should have known it!"

"Are you saying you knew she'd climb a chair to hang a mobile from the ceiling, instead of sticking to painting the lower areas?"

"*Hell*, no," he snapped. "I didn't begin to dream she'd...not at seven months..." He had no words to describe his feelings—none that wouldn't betray Jenny, at least.

With only traces of her own grief still lingering in her eyes, Laila frowned. "This is why you're so overprotective with this baby and me, isn't it?"

He couldn't read her tone, but for the first time she seemed to be asking without defiance or rancor. In simple relief he nodded, and buried his face in her hair.

Finally she turned a little, and kissed his forehead. "Thank you."

She was silent for a long time after that. They held each other in a peace they'd never achieved together before this moment.

Jake felt at peace. Laila had only asked a few questions. She didn't judge him, offered no platitudes, gave no advice. She just held him and let him feel as he did, let him be, and for the first time since Jen's death, the burden of guilt and dark silence wasn't weighing him down. He wasn't alone… and if he didn't deserve the gift she'd given him today, he'd still take it, clutch it to his chest with the greed of long abstinence from the human race. When had he deserved any of the sweet miracles he'd been given since meeting Laila?

He kissed her gently on the cheek. "Thank *you*, Laila."

She smiled at him, but it was tinged with sadness. No wonder, after the day they'd had, the pain they'd shared. "So what's next?"

The question took him by surprise. He frowned, and waited. He knew her well enough by now to know when she had something on her mind.

She surprised him again, by the quiet sorrow in her eyes as she waited.

Waited for him to speak.

After a long silence, he rasped, "What do you want from me?"

Her eyes shimmered with that sweet, disturbing sadness. She shook her head. "No, Jake. Not what I want. Not what's best for me, or for the baby. What do you want?"

He stared at her, his frown deepening. Why was she asking?

A tender hand closed his eyes. "Don't think, Jake. Just tell me what you want to do. First thing that comes to your mind."

The first thing that came to his mind? *No, no!* The very thought filled him with terror. He gripped her waist, trying to stop himself from shaking, but the tremors overtook him and wouldn't be denied. "No," he growled, closing his eyes against the pain. "No!"

"Then I'll say it for you." The sweet whisper sounded in his ear. "You want to go home. You need your family. You want to see her. You need to see her."

He scrambled out of her arms and off the bed, fury filling every part of him. *"No!"*

If the snarl took her aback, she didn't show it. "Have you been to see her, to see your daughter, since the funerals?"

Beyond words now, he held up a fisted hand to stop her—a command or plea, he no longer knew. At this moment, he didn't know anything except that he could never go back.

"If I was Jenny—if I died, and our baby—I'd want to be remembered," she said quietly. "I'd want you to come and see us, to remember and honor the love we shared."

His knees wouldn't hold him up. He landed on the ground before her, and grasped her arms. "You're not going to die. *You and this baby will not die!"*

Her mouth trembled, and she bit it down. She sat up; tender hands cupped his face. "This isn't about me, or this baby. It's about Jenny and Annabel—it will always be about Jenny and Annabel, and *why* you won't go to them."

"Stop. Please." He couldn't say any more.

"Someone has to, Jake. You won't let anyone else in, and you won't listen to your own heart, so it looks like it has to be me. *You need to go home.*"

Desperate to end this, he growled, "If you don't stop this I'll leave tonight and never come back!"

She smiled at him, with infinite sadness. "If you don't stop this, you'll never stop running anyway. I think I always knew you'd go one day."

He let go of her shoulders, and gripped the bedcover with fists so hard he could feel the tough fabric starting to tear.

Her palms moved tenderly over his unshaven jaw. "You've been resisting, fighting living again for so long, I think you've forgotten what the fight was about in the first place. Maybe if you go home, you'll find out."

He jerked his face from her hold; avoiding her welcoming lap, he dropped facedown onto the bedcovers. "I can't go home. I don't *deserve* to go home. I don't deserve to heal!"

After a short silence, the breath whooshed out of her; and that was the only sound for a very long time. He couldn't look up, refused to see the pity in her eyes—

"That has to be the most selfish thing I've ever heard."

Stunned, his head snapped up; and he saw, not compassion, but distinct exasperation in those expressive eyes. "What?"

"You heard me." With a well-aimed shove, she left him tumbling to the floor. "You said you were responsible for my mess? Look at the disasters in your own life before you take on the problems in mine, bud. I can look after myself and the baby. Stop hiding behind me. Grow up, John Jacob Sutherland. Be a man and face up to the past, and your responsibilities. Go home and see your sister and brother, who've been covering your butt the past five years. And go and see Jenny and Annabel while you're there."

Jake scrambled to his feet, chest heaving with his own fair measure of anger. "Yeah, sure, Dear Abby—and what's next? Saying goodbye to them, so I can heal and ride into the sunset with the pregnant princess?"

"Oh, give me a break! What makes you think any of this is about me—or about you, for that matter?" She rolled her eyes. "Right now I don't give a hang what *you* want, what you need or deserve—but your sister and brother, your *wife and daughter*, deserve far better than the nothing you've given them while you've run around the Outback in a self-hate party for one for the past five years!"

It was as if a sudden explosion blasted behind his eyes; pain roared through his solar plexus. Half-ready for escape, he took an instinctive step back, and gripped something behind him for balance as he absorbed the truth.

She was right.

Had he ever really thought about how Sandy and Aaron had coped the past five years? Had he ever seriously considered asking? No—it had all been about *him*. What he deserved—or didn't. He'd never once wondered how they were coping.

He'd lived like a hermit nomad the past five years to avoid the one thing he'd longed for and feared the most: going to Jenny's grave, and Annabel's.

He closed his eyes, and a single tear leaked from behind his right eye.

"Go," Laila said softly, her voice gentle. "Go to them."

"I can't," he rasped. "I can't do it, Laila. I—I don't know how to forget them. I can't say goodbye, or accept that they're never coming back…"

"Then don't," she whispered. "Just tell them the truth."

Another tear slipped down his cheek. He swiped at it. "What truth?" he asked huskily. He wasn't sure of anything at this moment.

"Tell them you're sorry," she said, very quietly. "Tell them you'd give anything to have them back." Her voice was almost gone now, but she kept speaking, rough with pain. "Tell them you'll never forget them." She paused for a few moments, then whispered so softly he had to strain to hear it. "Tell them you love them, and you always will."

CHAPTER ELEVEN

JAKE'S head bowed. He felt stripped bare, years of bitterness and self-hate exposed to her clear-eyed gaze—and worst, the *love*. This magnificent woman, the woman bearing his child, wouldn't fight for him. She knew he loved Jen, and accepted it with a dignity he hadn't found inside himself for too many years.

Slowly he nodded...and the acceptance of what he had to do washed over him like cool water over desert-heated skin. It was time.

"Go," she whispered. "Go now."

His eyes burning, he looked at her.

White and still, her eyes dark and red-rimmed, her bright hair a mess around her face, she had never looked more beautiful to him. Tears streaked her cheeks, but still she smiled, sweet and tremulous. "Go. We'll be fine."

"Come with me." He held out his hand to her.

She shook her head, smiling. "It's not my place. Just go."

Frowning, he muttered, "I want you to come with me." He wanted her to meet his family, wanted to bring his new life into the old. Wanted to marry her and make a family once again, without needing to say goodbye to the past.

But Laila shook her head once more, pressing her lips together for a moment before she smiled again. "Your family deserve to see you—Jenny deserves this, without me in the way."

Yes, she was right; yet his every instinct screamed against leaving her.

"Come with me. I want you to meet the family," he pressed, not knowing why, only that he couldn't bear the thought of going home without her beside him, giving him her fearless truth and unvarnished insights, showing him as the man he really was—and how he could be.

"No," she whispered again, her face white. "This is your life, Jake. Not mine."

A frisson of panic skittered through him. "It can be your life, Laila, if only you want it. The wedding, the home and kids…finishing your course." *Me. I'm offering you all that I am, all that I have.* She deserved all that and more, for everything she'd done for him.

For once she didn't seem to hear his internal cry, his silent call for her. She turned away, groping for her pillow, and hugging it to her. So lost, so fragile, yet her strength awed him over and over. "I can't."

"Why?"

He watched her gulp in a breath, as if she'd forgotten how until that moment. Not looking at him, she said in a rush, "You know why. I've told you so many times it must be boring."

Love. She wanted love. The one thing he still couldn't, maybe never could, give her.

Slowly her gaze came around to meet his. "You belong to her. Apart from the baby, I'm just a stepping stone on your path back home…aren't I, Jake?"

The look was steady, accepting—filled with an honesty that compelled his own. "You're far more than that. I—I care about you, Laila. I need you—and I'd be faithful—"

She tucked a mass of hair behind her ear. "I wish that could be enough." A little, hopeless shrug. "But I'm in love with you, Jake. I have been from the start." Her gaze dropped to the pillow; she nibbled on her thumbnail for a moment, while he stood there, feeling humble and awed and ashamed. "Go home, Jake. Be the man I always knew you could be."

"I don't want to go without you, Laila. I want you with me." He knew he was pleading now, but he didn't care; he needed Laila, *needed* her presence to feel like a whole man again. He knelt before her, and lifted her chin, trying to force her to look at him. "You said you'd marry me when I could say I *want* to marry you. I'm saying it. I want to marry you, and not just for the baby. I want you with me for life."

She wouldn't meet his eyes. "I must have lied," she mumbled. "I didn't know then. But I can't imagine worse torture than living in your home, where she was—where she'll always be a part of your heart."

His straight-down-the-line Laila was changing the rules on him? He jerked back, letting go of her chin. "I thought you understood my feelings for her. I thought—"

"I do," she cried, fierce with restrained passion. "She should be part of your heart. I could never begrudge her that—but it's harder to take when you don't—when you don't love me. I— I can't endure years of watching you trying so hard to give me what you don't have." Her little, gulping sob left a physical ache in Jake's throat. "I'll let you know when the baby's born, all right? I've never asked you for anything. Please, just go!"

She was ready to cry, and he couldn't do a thing about it. Helpless, frustrated and wishing he could give her everything she hadn't asked for, he kissed her cheek, and said, gently yet with the force of a vow, "I'm coming back for you, Laila. I'm coming back."

She shook her head and buried her face in the pillow, no longer caring if he saw her cry or not, or she couldn't wait any more for him to leave her in peace.

Jake got to his feet and walked out of the room on unsteady feet, feeling like a stranger in a world he thought he'd known.

* * *

From her window, dry-eyed and calm, Laila watched the family light plane take off an hour later.

He'd taken the family plane. He'd meant what he'd said. He was coming back.

Coming back to me.

Or he thought so, now—and he probably would come back. There was the baby to consider—but he hadn't yet been home. He hadn't seen his family…or told his long-dead yet still beloved wife what he needed to say.

She wondered, briefly, like a coward, if she could stay in this room for the next few days or weeks, until she could tell the family what they were waiting to hear without breaking down. She felt so lost, so *alone*.

The baby kicked, a soft, bubbling flutter.

Laila smiled and caressed her tummy. "I know, little one. You're here, and I love you." *But I love your daddy, too, and he's leaving—*

She closed her eyes as the familiar stinging returned.

A soft knock sounded at the door. Laila sighed, gathered up her courage and resolve and said, "Come in."

Dar's face popped around the door. "Hey, Princess."

"Hey," she replied huskily.

He smiled at her. "Thought you'd want to know, Tom Appleyard rang up just now. Said the foal's drinking well, and standing without assistance. The surrogate mare's accepted her, and she's accepted the mare."

Joy and sorrow mixed in her heart, like a bittersweet cocktail of loss and healing, hurting and yet right. And she smiled back. "That's good news."

He didn't come into her room, but remained at the half-closed door. "Dave Randall said it's been a hard summer and autumn for him. He wanted to know if you'd consider work experience for the next couple of months. You'd be his assistant, doing the smaller jobs for now, but leaving him free for the hardest stuff."

"Sounds like exactly what I need right now, like a gift from heaven…or maybe not," she added, suddenly suspicious. "Be honest, Dar. Did Dave call here, or did you call him?" She watched her father closely.

Her father's twitching grin gave him away. "Well, Dave jumped at the idea…"

And though she thought it would take a long time to laugh again, she found herself chuckling. "You're a shocker, you know that?"

He shrugged. "Can't help myself, Princess—but I am trying to let go." Staying at the door he asked, with obvious diffidence, "You…okay?"

Her anxious, overprotective Dar was giving her space, asking without demanding. A long-overdue acknowledgment of her maturity, and her right to make her own decisions. The tears spilled over again before she could control them, but she smiled. "No, Dar, I'm not okay—but I will be."

She opened her arms, and her father came to her, an equal for the first time.

Moments later, the small, winking light of the light plane faded into the distance, and disappeared.

This was all wrong.

The deep darkness of a cool autumn night over Burrabilla was punctuated by the lights of every car on the place, turned on and facing each other every fifty meters or so in a makeshift runway.

This was the welcoming party he wished he could have avoided. He'd wanted, more than anything, to see only Sandy and Aaron first, or better yet, go to Jenny's and Annabel's graves before going home at all; he wanted to ease back into the life he'd left behind. But it was dark and this wasn't his plane, so he had to radio his arrival in.

He should have put the trip off until morning—but he knew if he'd put it off, he wouldn't have been able to leave Laila at all.

He was circling the home paddock now, ready for landing, his heart sad and full, his stomach clenching with joy and terror. How could this homecoming feel so right, and so wrong, at once? He was finally home. How could he feel so *torn*?

Laila's face rose in his mind, sassy and pert, strong and lost. *I'm in love with you, but you don't love me. She'll always be in your heart.*

He had to block Laila from his mind, or he'd go crazy—or turn back to get her.

He thought of his brother and sister. Sandy and Aaron's joyous excitement at hearing his voice put a lump in his throat that was still there now, an hour later; but hearing his mother's voice, seeing her at Burrabilla at all, wasn't something he was looking forward to.

Who was he to judge who belonged here or didn't? Sandy and Aaron had that right. They'd done all the hard work, facing up to their responsibilities while he'd done just what Laila had said: ran around the country in a self-hate party for one.

That has to be the most selfish thing I've ever heard. What makes you think any of this is about you?

He smiled, just thinking about it. Lord help him, but he needed that woman! Only hours had passed, but he missed her already, missed her fearless honesty and sweet teasing, her love and her—

He missed her love? Was he the most selfish man on the face of the earth, wanting to keep the love of the amazing woman who was having his child while unable to give it back?

Or did it mean something more?

He shook his head. Whatever it was, now wasn't the time. He could just imagine Laila's eyes, all warm and teasing, as she told him to get his priorities straight…and she'd be right.

He stopped stalling, and got the landing gear in place, and was on the ground within two minutes.

Sandy was pulling the door open before he'd even turned the engine off. "Jake! Oh, *Jake*, thank God you're home…" She'd flung herself into his arms and burst into tears while he was still only halfway out of the plane.

"Hey, San, you're choking me," he mock complained past the thickness in his throat. He wrapped his arms around his sister and held her close. "Sheesh, anyone would think you hadn't seen me in years."

A knuckle-punch on his deltoid brought back a ton of memories, and he grinned at his brother. "Ow. Watch it, Az, you're stronger than you used to be."

"That's kinda the point." Aaron grinned back. "Leave me with all the ruddy work for five years, will ya?"

He tried to clear his throat, failed and spoke through the lump. "Yeah, well, about that, I know I should have…"

"Stop it," Sandy cried, kissing his cheek. "You did it for us for twelve years, Jake."

"Don't even think it, mate, or you'll cop another knuckle-punch. Even when we could've killed you, we understood, so don't you apologize. We don't need it." Aaron spoke with the kind of ferocity that had always been alien to his nature—but then, when they'd all lived here together, Sandy hadn't been given to bouts of tears or hanging on to him, either. She was the tough Outback chick who could do anything the boys could do, and frequently do it better; Aaron was the family dreamer, and he, Jake, had taken care of them.

Seemed the past five years had changed more than him alone.

"Of course they understand. You were their mother and father for so many years after I left you all."

Without a word, Sandy and Aaron moved aside at the sound of the tired voice: the fluid, musical voice he'd only rarely heard in the past twenty or more years. The voice he barely knew, because he'd refused to go with the kids on visitation weekends to Brisbane. Someone had had to stay home with their father to help with the workload.

He'd had to make sure poor old Dad made it through the weekends without jumping in the plane with the kids, to beg his wife for one more chance...a chance she wouldn't give him. She'd been a city girl who hated the Outback life, and his father's spirit would wither and die in a three-bedroom house on a quarter-acre block in the suburbs. They'd married after a brief affair that left her pregnant with Jake—but as Laila had proven to him with her graphic account of her friend Danni's parents, some marriages just didn't work.

"I'll go back inside if you prefer, Jake."

Jake looked around. Standing still and straight behind them, tall and graceful, lovely in the timeless way of Eurasian women, his mother watched the reunion with an impassive glance...the same impassivity he'd used himself the past five years to shield himself from pain.

With all his stubborn will, he tried to hang on to the hurts of the past, to see his dad's utter loneliness—to remember the years of sacrifice he'd made to raise his brother and sister, but he couldn't do it. He needed the forgiveness his brother and sister had given so freely after he'd deserted them, ran from his responsibilities.

Like mother, like son.

"Hello, Mum," he said quietly, the long-unused word feeling strange on his tongue. "I'd welcome you home, but I think the shoe's on the wrong foot for that."

Mai smiled at her son. "Then I'll welcome you." She came forward with a hesitant step.

He really wasn't ready for this—but as Aaron and Sandy moved away, giving Mai room, he bent a little, and allowed her to kiss his cheek.

The awkwardness of the touch couldn't be helped; he'd barely seen her in twenty years, choosing to take sides, refusing to forgive one for the pain of the other.

With a man's eyes—the eyes of a man given redemption freely—his vision had cleared.

"Well, are we going to stand around shivering here all night, or get inside?" Aaron demanded. Answering his own question, he reached in and shouldered Jake's backpack.

As they began walking toward the homestead, various long-time workers slapped Jake on the back or murmured affectionate insults—a typical Australian welcome-home. The women hugged him as a long-lost child.

Maybe there was more to this prodigal son business than he'd thought.

"Bill and Adah will be here for lunch," Sandy said, leading the way inside the house. "Darren will be over with his wife, Lucy, for dinner. They're so excited you're finally home."

Jake stilled. His parents-in-law, and brother-in-law? It was too much, far too much!

Mai, who'd been walking beside him, said softly, "It'll hurt for a long time, until you find the echoes of all this forgiveness inside yourself." She nodded as he looked, startled, down at her. "I could give lectures on self-hate, and you are far more my son than you want to be." She hesitated as they reached the kitchen, where, by the smell of things, a pot of tea and a chocolate cake awaited them. "Maybe we could talk about it later?"

He couldn't think of anything to say in response. It had never occurred to him that his mother, of all people, could understand him so well.

But then, it had never occurred to him that a red-haired Outback girl with a sassy mouth and the heart of a wild brumby, who didn't know the meaning of the word *no*, could bring him back to his family, to the joy of living, either.

At thirty-eight, Jake realized, he still had a lot to learn about life—but finally, at last, he was willing to learn.

He smiled at Mai, and said, just as soft, "I'd like that."

CHAPTER TWELVE

"HI, JEN," Jake said, in a strangled kind of whisper. "Bet you thought I'd never get here."

Finally, after almost a week at Burrabilla, everyone had had their share of seeing him, he'd worked his land and come to some kind of peace with his former in-laws. Now, at last he had time, in the quiet hours before sunset, to come.

To her…to *them*. Jenny and Annabel.

He walked quietly past the grave of his father and grandparents to the small, fenced-in graves of his wife and daughter. He'd stopped to pick some of the hardy perennial flowers his mother had recently planted around the veranda, and separated them into two bunches. Not much of an apology, he knew, but what could possibly make up for ignoring his own wife and child for five years?

Somehow he'd expected the graves—one adult-size, one so pitifully tiny—to be wild and overgrown: a silent testimony to his neglect. He should have known Sandy better than that. While they hadn't been seen to for about a week, and the flowers were faded now, most of the weeds were new growth.

Grateful to have something physical to do, he began pulling out the lamb's-tongue and the dandelions, focusing his thoughts on that and just letting himself talk.

"I'm glad Sandy's been taking care of you both. I've been

gone a long time, I know—but I'm back, Jen. You probably always knew I'd run, didn't you? You always said I was like my mother, whenever we had a fight. Well, I can't run anymore, Jen. I'm tired, and I want to come home. I want to stay." He gave a wry smile. "I can almost see you smiling at me. I always blathered on when I got nervous, didn't I? Laila would laugh to hear that. She wouldn't believe—" He skidded to a halt. What was he doing, talking about Laila at Jen's grave?

Then he smiled again, because somehow it felt *right* to tell her.

"Laila's the reason I'm here now, Jen. She's an extraordinary person. You'd like her." He gulped down the burning ball of pain in his throat. "Jen, I—" he dragged in a breath, closed his eyes and blurted out all the things he'd been holding in for five years "—oh, dear God, I'm sorry, Jen. I shouldn't have left you that day. I should have taken you to your parents', instead of letting you convince me to stay home. If I'd been thinking about anything but the cattle and profit-loss, I'd have known you'd drag out a stupid ladder or chair to finish Annabel's room. You could never stand being bored, could you, darlin'?"

With the long-unused endearment, the first tear sprung up, and ran down his face: it felt cold as ice with the breeze frolicking around him. "I'm so sorry, Jen, so *sorry*... I'd give *anything* if it hadn't happened—if you and Annabel were here with me now, and the other kids we'd planned together."

Though he was saying the words Laila had given him, not one of them was scripted. Everything came from inside his long-frozen heart.

And yet he couldn't go on, for it wasn't true. It had been true, a few months ago—it had even felt true three days ago—*but now it wasn't*. He'd loved Jen so deeply, with a love he'd been sure would last a lifetime. A big part of him still loved her, and always would; but would he truly give *anything* to have her back?

No, he wouldn't give anything. Not anymore.

And slowly, he smiled through the tears that wouldn't stop falling. "I can't lie—not to you, Jen. I'll always love you—you know that—and if you were still alive, I wouldn't be thinking this, or saying it. I wouldn't have met her. But something's happened to me I never expected. I couldn't give anything to have you here…not anymore. You see, I'm going to be a daddy again. I've been watching him grow inside Laila, and I've felt him kick. And I just *know* that when he's out in the world, and he smiles at me, I'm going to turn to mush…just like I do when Laila's near me."

Laila…sunshine Laila with her hair in its scrabbled ponytail, freckled nose and sassy mouth, and a heart that didn't know the meaning of the word no—but she knew all about healing one stubborn, stupid jackaroo who hadn't wanted to live.

"I love her, Jen," he whispered, in sudden, blinding wonder. "I didn't know—I couldn't stand the thought of loving any woman but you for so long that when I met her, even though I couldn't stop looking at her, I didn't realize what it meant. But she took me as I was—a complete jerk who did nothing but hurt her—and she loves me.

"She loves me," he said softly, smiling. "Maybe you wouldn't wonder at that, but I know it for the miracle it is. I've spent years running scared from getting close to anyone, in case they died, too. I would never have given Laila a chance, but for the baby. She opened her heart to me, and I kept pushing her away. She never stopped giving to me, Jen, and never once asked for anything back. If she hadn't kept the baby…if I hadn't found her that day in the barn, she might have disappeared without ever telling me, and I wouldn't be here now, back with the family. I would never have come home, but for her. I wouldn't be me again, but for her."

He bowed his head for a minute, eyes closed, breathing in the scent of home, the essence of being here at Burrabilla, where he belonged. Thinking of how his life would be now, if he'd walked away from Wallaby and Laila.

"I need her, Jen. I need her with me, my wife, the mother of my children. I know you'd understand that—but you and Annabel will always be here with us."

He dropped to his knees, and after tossing out the wilted flowers in the vases resting on the headstones, replaced them with the fresh ones he'd picked. He picked up the plucked weeds, and tossed them away.

His fingers brushed over the gold lettering on the dark marble. *Jennifer Connors Sutherland, beloved wife and mother. Annabel Adah Sutherland, beloved daughter.* His hand lingered over the tiny grave of his daughter, his firstborn, now and always.

He would never forget them…and because of the miracle of a woman who loved him, he knew he didn't have to. Laila accepted that his first wife and child would always be part of his heart—but the love they'd shared enriched the life he chose now. A life with Laila, his beautiful, feisty, stubborn, adorable Outback woman, who loved him with all her giving heart…and who might take more than a little convincing to believe in him, the way he believed in her.

"I'll be back," he vowed to them both, as he got back to his feet. "And this time, it's a promise I'll keep."

Without stopping at Burrabilla—he'd radio the family from the air, and make them the same promise he'd just made to Jen and Annabel—he sprinted for the plane.

"Thanks for that, Laila. It saves me from hours more on a— messy job," Dave Randall said, flinging a friendly arm around Laila's shoulders as they alighted from the four-wheel-drive at Wallaby.

She grinned up at him. "Messy being the operative word." She mock-shuddered. "Four hours of shaving Tilda Braun's sheep's bums. Has anyone told you lately that pregnant women are subject to bouts of nausea?"

"It's called *crutching*," Dave informed her, mock-haughtily, "and besides, Tilda deserves the help, coping alone with four kids and the sheep run since Pete's death. You took on the job like a real pro."

As expected, she chuckled. Everyone was trying so hard to cheer her up. "Ah, can the flattery, Dave. Nothing you say or do will make me take that job on a regular basis."

"Yes, you would," Dave said softly, and, swiping her hat, he ruffled her already messy and probably stinking hair, after spending the entire afternoon shaving the back ends of the sheep, and clearing out any traces of infection. Crutching was one of the most boring, messy and smelly jobs an Outback vet had to handle. Most owners did the job themselves; but Tilda Braun had had to let as many of her workers go as she could after her husband's death, and the insurance payout hadn't been a tenth of what they'd paid for.

The Braun job wasn't the only freebie job she'd done. She'd had plenty of pro bono experience this week. Everyone in the region suddenly had jobs for her, and as they cheerfully explained, since they didn't have to pay her, they might as well "make use of the sheila."

At least sheila was an upgrade on "the Princess", she thought wryly. It seemed there was one upside to having her heart… dented. People were seeing her as a real person. Nobody was bothering with gossip about her spending so much time with the hunky, blond, single vet. And keeping busy all day left her too exhausted at night to stay awake and grieve for losing Jake.

For much longer than an hour or two, anyway.

But when she was brutally honest with herself, she knew she had no right to grieve. Jake was probably happy now, back in the bosom of his family, safe and busy in the role he'd been born and bred for—and he'd never truly been hers to lose. This was the wages of her sin the night of Dar and Marcie's party, in taking what she'd never been given the right to have.

"Oy, Robbins, where'd your head wander off to just now—and without your hat—?"

Caught out in near-tears yet again, she forced a smile and lunged awkwardly at Dave as he danced away, laughing, with her Akubra. "Hey, give me that hat, Randall. It might be old and dented, but it's hiding the sheep poop—"

"Laila."

That voice, deep and dark as night... With a gasp, she whirled around.

A man stood on the lengthening shadows on the veranda.

He even made stillness and silence a thing of beauty and enthrallment.

One step, another; walking toward a promise of heaven she'd always known was out of reach, but she couldn't help herself. She couldn't speak, couldn't tear her gaze from him.

Vaguely she heard Dave's four-wheel-drive starting up and driving off. It didn't matter. He was here...Jake had come back...

He stepped out of the dimness and into the last rays of daylight, into the riot of sunset colors. Down one stair, another, his gaze locked on her, as if, disheveled and covered with mud and sheep dung, she was still exquisite to him.

He stood a step away from her, drinking in her face. His nose crinkled up as he put his hands on her shoulders. "You stink, Robbins," he said softly, with a smile...a thing of beauty and simplicity—a smile without shadows, at last.

This was the man she'd ached to know from the first day.

The tips of her mouth curved up as she found words—typical Laila words for this profound moment. "Been crutching—you know, shaving sheep's bums—all afternoon."

He grinned, and touched her face with the kind of tenderness she'd only known from him the day she'd had the cramps. "That's my woman. Can't cook to save her life, doesn't know a vacuum cleaner from a tractor, but she's always ready to jump down into her favorite kind of war zone."

She gasped, choked and went into a fit of uncontrollable coughing.

She only realized she was in his arms when the gentle, surging heel-of-palm pats to her back soothed the choking, and his lips kissed away the tears streaming down her face. "Yeah, I said you're *my* woman," he growled in her ear, "smart mouth, sheep poop and all."

He tipped up her face to his. "*Believe*, Laila," he whispered as he bent to kiss her—long, deep, exquisitely, indescribably tender, filled with love. Laila, dazed and happy, could only kiss him back with all the love she'd tried to lock inside her heart for so long.

When he finally moved back an inch, she swayed into him, her head falling to his chest. She listened to his heart beating, solid, steady—here. Unbelievably *here*.

Believe, Laila.

She put a hand over his chest, feeling him breathe.

"I'm here, Laila—and I'm not going anywhere again without you. Well, maybe to the occasional stock sale or muster," he amended with a smile in his voice, "but not till this little guy's at least crawling around safely, and you've finished your degree." He kissed her again, and caressed her belly. "You look tired, sweetheart," he murmured. "I hear you haven't been sleeping much lately. You haven't been crying, have you? I told you I was coming back for you."

Aching with hope, she looked up at him. "Jake, I—"

He put a tender finger to her mouth. "You need the words? Believe, Laila. Believe in how amazing and lovable you are, just as you always believed you could heal me. I wasted so much time being afraid I'd lose you, I almost did—but I'm not afraid anymore," he said, very softly, smiling at her with all the tenderness she'd ever dreamed of. "I think I loved you all along, just like you love me. You're a very smart woman, you know that? You sent me back to Burrabilla to face my ghosts—but they were all in my mind. Everyone had forgiven me, but me. I needed to go home to see what you already knew—that giving up on life and love was only dishonoring her memory." He kissed her again. "Will you marry me, Laila? Will you marry the dumb goof who was too blind to see the priceless treasure right in front of him?"

His eyes were luminous with love, making her heart turn over in her chest. "Oh, Jake…"

Smiling, he pushed his finger down over her mouth. "Keep that sassy mouth for kissing. It's finally my turn to talk. I got your family to fly to town for a meal. I figure we have about—" he checked his watch "—another two hours before your dad can't take the wait anymore, and comes back to see what's going on."

With a twitching smile, she nodded against his finger.

"Good. I'll draw you a bubble bath. Marcie's made a meal fit for a princess. While I set it up, you go and soak out, wash your hair, get dressed in your prettiest maternity dress and come back down. I refuse to be accepted by a woman covered in mud and sheep's dags."

And, as if to prove how offended he really was, he kissed her again…

EPILOGUE

Bathurst, three years later

"LAILA SUTHERLAND."

Thunderous applause came from the back rows as, gowned and capped, and grinning fit to burst a blood vessel, Laila walked up the stairs to accept her degree.

Laila Sutherland, Bachelor of Veterinary Science.

She'd made it at last. They'd spent the past year here in Bathurst as she finished her degree, and made it with honors. Tomorrow, they were heading back to Burrabilla for good.

They were going home.

Once she'd taken her degree from the dean, she turned and held it up with a triumphant grin. Her gaze locked in on her people. Dar and Marcie, bouncing in their seats; Mai, smiling and waving at her; Drew and Glenn, Aaron and Sandy all hooting, clapping and whistling in pride.

Jimmy was there, too, hooting and stamping his feet. His latest girlfriend sat beside him—Chelle, or Shana, or something like that. She couldn't keep a list of the country girls who threw themselves at him on a regular basis. Handsome, single country vets were in short supply...

Danni and Jodie were there, waving and hollering, "Laila! Laila!"

Even Dave Randall had made the trek from home, and was grinning in pride. He'd kept her on track during the six months they'd stayed at Wallaby before and after Ally's birth, keeping up her reading—and using her skills on a regular basis. She hadn't wanted to at first, but Jake insisted that he was Ally's daddy and he was perfectly capable of caring for their daughter while she got her career on track.

And he'd done exactly that the past year, being the full-time daddy, cooking and cleaning and caring for the family while Laila concentrated on her final year.

Her gaze came to the front row where her beloved Jake sat, with dark-haired, blue-eyed, adorable Ally Jennifer Sutherland on his lap, in her prettiest blue dress and the pink patent shoes she insisted on wearing everywhere, waving at her mummy.

When, after sixteen hours of labor, Dr. Broughton had said the timeless words, "It's a girl," she'd been too exhausted for shock—and too happy to have her beautiful little girl to care. Jake had been over the moon, and totally wrapped around Ally's finger from the moment of her birth—but that didn't stop him teasing Laila unmercifully about her woeful mother's instinct.

He asked her constantly to predict the sex of the baby she carried now; but she'd learned her lesson. A prophetess she was not. One very happy wife to her adoring husband, and mother to the most beautiful child in the world—not to mention Burrabilla's new qualified vet—would do her, any day.

* * * * *

Silhouette® Romantic Suspense keeps getting hotter!

Turn the page for a sneak preview of
New York Times *bestselling author*
Beverly Barton's latest title
from THE PROTECTORS *miniseries.*

HIS ONLY OBSESSION
by Beverly Barton

On sale March 2007 wherever books are sold.

Gwen took a taxi to the Yellow Parrot, and with each passing block she grew more tense. It didn't take a rocket scientist to figure out that this dive was in the worst part of town. Gwen had learned to take care of herself, but the minute she entered the bar, she realized that a smart woman would have brought a gun with her. The interior was hot, smelly and dirty, and the air was so smoky that it looked as if a pea soup fog had settled inside the building. Before she had gone three feet, an old drunk came up to her and asked for money. Sidestepping him, she searched for someone who looked as if he or she might actually work here, someone other than the prostitutes who were trolling for customers.

After fending off a couple of grasping young men and ignoring several vulgar propositions in an odd mixture of Spanish and English, Gwen found the bar. She ordered a beer from the burly, bearded bartender. When he set the beer in front of her, she took the opportunity to speak to him.

"I'm looking for a man. An older American man, in his seventies. He was probably with a younger woman. This man is my father and—"

"*No hablo inglés.*"

"Oh." He didn't speak English and she didn't speak Spanish. Now what?

While she was considering her options, Gwen noticed a young man in skintight black pants and an open black shirt, easing closer and closer to her as he made his way past the other men at the bar.

Great. That was all she needed—some horny young guy mistaking her for a prostitute.

"*Señorita*." His voice was softly accented and slightly slurred. His breath smelled of liquor. "You are all alone, *sí?*"

"Please, go away," Gwen said. "I'm not interested."

He laughed, as if he found her attitude amusing. "Then it is for me to make you interested. I am Marco. And you are...?"

"Leaving," Gwen said.

She realized it had been a mistake to come here alone tonight. Any effort to unearth information about her father in a place like this was probably pointless. She would do better to come back tomorrow and try to speak to the owner. But when she tried to move past her ardent young suitor, he reached out and grabbed her arm. She tensed.

Looking him right in the eyes, she told him, "Let go of me. Right now."

"But you cannot leave. The night is young."

Gwen tugged on her arm, trying to break free. He tightened his hold, his fingers biting into her flesh. With her heart beating rapidly as her basic fight-or-flight instinct kicked in, she glared at the man.

"I'm going to ask you one more time to let me go."

Grinning smugly, he grabbed her other arm, holding her in place.

Suddenly, seemingly from out of nowhere, a big hand clamped down on Marco's shoulder, jerked him back and spun him around. Suddenly free, Gwen swayed slightly but managed to retain her balance as she watched in amazement as a tall, lanky man in jeans and cowboy boots shoved her would-be suitor up against the bar.

"I believe the lady asked you real nice to let her go," the man said, in a deep Texas drawl. "Where I come from, a gentleman respects a lady's wishes."

Marco grumbled something unintelligible in Spanish. Probably cursing, Gwen thought. Or maybe praying. If she were Marco, she would be praying that the big, rugged American wouldn't beat her to a pulp.

Apparently Marco was not as smart as she was. When the Texan released him, he came at her rescuer, obviously intending to fight him. The Texan took Marco out with two swift punches, sending the younger man to the floor. Gwen glanced down at where Marco lay sprawled flat on his back, unconscious.

Her hero turned to her. "Ma'am, are you all right?"

She nodded. The man was about six-two, with a sunburned tan, sun-streaked brown hair and azure-blue eyes.

"What's a lady like you doing in a place like this?" he asked.

REQUEST YOUR FREE BOOKS!
2 FREE NOVELS PLUS 2
FREE GIFTS!

HARLEQUIN ROMANCE®

From the Heart, For the Heart

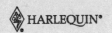

HARLEQUIN®

EVERLASTING LOVE™

Every great love has a story to tell™

Save $1.⁰⁰ off

**the purchase of
any Harlequin
Everlasting Love novel**

Coupon valid from January 1, 2007
until April 30, 2007.

Valid at retail outlets in the U.S. only.
Limit one coupon per customer.

5 65373 00076 2   (8100) 0 11302

HEUSCPN0407

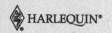

E V E R L A S T I N G L O V E ™

Every great love has a story to tell™

Save $1.⁰⁰ off

the purchase of
any Harlequin
Everlasting Love novel

Coupon valid from January 1, 2007
until April 30, 2007.

Valid at retail outlets in Canada only.
Limit one coupon per customer.

52607370

HECDNCPN0407

This February...

Catch NASCAR Superstar **Carl Edwards** *in*

SPEED DATING!

Kendall assesses risk for a living—
so she's the last person you'd
expect to see on the arm of a
race-car driver who thrives on the
unpredictable. But when a bizarre
turn of events—and NASCAR
hotshot Dylan Hargreave—inspire
her to trade in her ever-so-structured
existence for "life in the fast lane"
she starts to feel she might be
on to something!

**Collect all 4 debut novels in
the Harlequin NASCAR series.**

SPEED DATING
by *USA TODAY* bestselling author
Nancy Warren

THUNDERSTRUCK
by Roxanne St. Claire

HEARTS UNDER CAUTION
by Gina Wilkins

DANGER ZONE
by Debra Webb

*On sale
February
2007*

Hearts racing
Blood pumping
Pulses accelerating

Falling in love can be a blur…especially at **180 mph!**

So if you crave the thrill of the chase—on and off the track—you'll love

SPEED DATING
by **Nancy Warren!**

Hearts racing
Blood pumping
Pulses accelerating

Falling in love can be a blur...especially at
180 mph!

So if you crave the thrill of the chase—on and off the track—you'll love
SPEED DATING
by Nancy Warren!

Coming Next Month